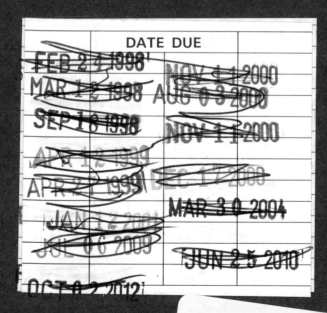

a stranger in this world

kevin canty

PUBLISHED BY DOUBLEDAY
a division of Bantam Doubleday Dell
Publishing Group, Inc. 1540 Broadway,
New York, New York 10036

DOUBLEDAY and the portrayal of an anchor
with a dolphin are trademarks of Doubleday, a division of Bantam Doubleday Dell
Publishing Group, Inc.

King of the Elephants was originally published in the *New England Review*'s Summer
1994 issue. © 1994 by Kevin Canty.

The Victim was originally published in *Esquire* magazine's July 1992 issue. © 1992
by Kevin Canty.

Moonbeams and Aspirin was originally published in *Story* magazine's Winter 1993
issue. © 1993 by Kevin Canty.

Blue Boy was originally published in the
Missouri Review's Winter 1994 issue.
© 1994 by Kevin Canty.

Great Falls, 1966 was originally published
in *Cut Bank*'s issue #41. © 1994 by Kevin
Canty.

Book design by Jennifer Ann Daddio

Library of Congress Cataloging-in-
Publication Data
Canty, Kevin.
A stranger in this world / by Kevin
Canty. — 1st ed.
p.   cm.
I. Title.
PS3553.A56S7   1994
813'.54—dc20   93-50609
CIP

ISBN 0-385-47387-7

for lucy, of course

contents

a stranger in this world

king of the elephants

THE THIRD TIME WE PUT MY MOTHER INTO THE HOSPITAL, MY father and I had already moved to Florida, to Jacksonville Beach. A cop called from D.C. at eleven o'clock one Friday night, said they'd found her sleeping on the subway, drunk, with a broken arm. Broken for at least two days, the cop said; she couldn't remember where or how. I remember looking at the wallpaper in our kitchen, just staring: gold diamonds with black flowerpots in the middle of them.

"When will we see you?" the cop asked. I heard the accusation in his voice, as always.

"We'll either be there tomorrow or we won't," I told him. "My father isn't here right now."

"Look," he said, losing his patience, but I hung up on him. I didn't feel like being scolded by a cop. In a minute the phone started to ring again and I let it.

I went out on the patio and sat there, resting, trying to get my energy up for whatever was going to happen next. I was filled with this enormous lethargy, as if my arms and legs all weighed hundreds of pounds. It was like being filled with water. I should have had some big emotion, shame or sorrow or guilt, but I didn't, maybe because this wasn't the first time or even the second. In some ways this wasn't even as bad as the second time, when she'd cut a man, a stranger to her, with the neck of a broken bottle.

For a while I thought of driving down to Anastasia Island —I could smoke some pot with the surfers down there, sleep on the beach. I didn't need this. I wondered what would happen if I didn't tell my father at all. There was nothing we could do anyway, nothing that would keep her out of trouble. I thought about what it was going to be like to see her. My mother always cleaned up nicely. A doctor had told me that once, and it stuck with me, because it was true. By the time we saw her the next day she would have paid an attendant to buy her a decent nightgown, and some ordinary clothes to leave the hospital in, blue jeans and a sweatshirt, something like that.

She would have had a shower, would have combed her hair and cut her nails and washed behind her ears. She'd smile at my father when he came in, but especially at me, would hold her arms out and wait for me to fill them, and she would hold me close and she might cry, and my mother would smell of shampoo and water and deodorant soap. If you saw her on the street you would see an ordinary woman, or slightly more interesting than ordinary: one of those well-off, independent women who approach their fifties in sneakers and naturally graying hair. You might suspect her of bird-watching, of having a VISUALIZE PEACE bumper sticker on her station wagon. You wouldn't imagine her naked on the bus, inviting the driver to fuck her. You wouldn't think she had a knife in her purse, defense against a conspiracy she wouldn't name, afraid to say the words.

After a little while I'd had enough of thinking. It wasn't going to make any difference. I threw a few clothes of mine and a few clothes of my father's into a gym bag, searched out a couple of hundred dollars in twenties from between the pages of my big yellow Babar book, king of the elephants, the only souvenir that I had left from my childhood. I knew he kept his walking-around money there. We were living like soldiers, my father and I, men thrown together without any secrets. I decided to drive over to the Tally-Ho, though it was only five or six blocks; it would save our coming back here, the endless fussing of my father when he was drunk. I knew what he would want to do.

I spotted his suit at the TV end of the bar, watching a ball game with a couple of other men, listening to a story. These suits—he had five or six of them, in green and tan and gray— were his invisible uniform, urban camouflage, and when we used to live in Washington they worked. He could just disappear into a crowd of suits, bald men with briefcases, but here in Florida he stood out like a pigeon in a crowd of peacocks.

"Dad," I said, taking the stool at his elbow.

He looked up, tired-looking, and saw my face in the mirror behind the bar. He started to smile but my face must have tipped him off. His smile vanished. He said, "It's Ellen, right? What is it this time?"

You see how it worked. We passed her around like the black queen in a game of hearts, the cops to the hospital, the hospital to my father, my father to me. I was the one who could not pass her on. I laid out the situation for him, as painlessly as I could, but the hard parts of the story could not be avoided: the subway, the two-days-broken arm. "They're holding her in St. Elizabeth's now," I told him, "but she can leave anytime she wants. There's nothing they can charge her with."

"She'll leave tomorrow," he said, turning from the mirror to look into my real face. But I kept my eyes on the mirror, watched him turn. "She'll go, don't you think?"

"She did before," I said.

"Then we have to get her," he said, and in this sentence everything was decided. He brought us to Florida, not so much to start a new life as to get away from the old one, and now the old life had caught up with us again. We both knew it would, I think. Maybe everything had already been decided. My father turned toward the mirror, smiled at my reflection in a resigned way, shrugged his shoulders. But it felt like this was a canned look, something he'd been practicing, I don't know.

"Let me finish my drink," he said softly. "We have time, I

think. Do you want anything? A Shirley Temple? I bet Karl would give you a beer."

"That's all right. I'll have a Coke."

"A Coke!" he said, like it was the greatest idea in the world. "Karl! Bring Raymond here a Coke." He turned toward me and dropped his voice. "You'll take the first shift driving, won't you? I'm a little sleepy. I'll catch a little shut-eye in the back, be good as new in a couple of hours. There's a game on —you can listen to the game."

The bartender set a Coke on the bar in front of me and a fresh gin and tonic in front of my father. I never saw him order it—a tilt of his head, a raised eyebrow, some signal the bartender understood. He drank gin in the summer and Manhattans in the winter. His glass looked clear and inviting, and it seemed to give off a faint phosphorescence, a glow, like a picture of a saint. We turned to the game but I couldn't hold my interest in it, the Padres and somebody else, one of those late West Coast games that don't even seem to matter to the players. I looked around the bar, curious. It was the first time I'd ever been in one of my father's places for any length of time. Everyone seemed friendly enough, and the darkness of the place was pleasant, but I didn't understand what would bring people out of their houses to come here. It was a comfortable, quiet kind of a bar anyway, with a jar of pickled eggs on the counter, Slim Jim sausages, potato chips and those little foil packs of aspirin. A few couples scattered among the tables, a knot of men at the back drinking beer and laughing, jet-butts from the naval air station most likely. I sat on my barstool, sipping my Coke, wondering why my father chose to spend his life here.

After a minute or two, a surprisingly short time, his glass was empty and we were saying good night. In the air of the parking lot was the damp salt kiss of the Atlantic. This part of town was all asphalt, strip malls and three-story apartment complexes, but you always knew the water wasn't far.

My father said a strange thing when we got outside. He looked around at the night, at the low, dull clouds in the sky, and said, "I wish I knew who you loved, Raymond."

I looked at him. I couldn't think of what to say. I heard the accusation in his voice, but I didn't know if I was guilty or not, and I didn't care. I was already as full of guilt as I was going to get. And these lunges toward honesty were never my father's best moments. When he was drunk the world and all the people in it appeared to him in bright primary colors of love and hate.

"It's just that you're so quiet," he finally said. "It's a good way to be—quiet. I never have been able to carry it off."

"I brought you some clothes," I told him, trying to change the subject.

He looked at me like I'd slapped him, leaning on the hood of our old Plymouth.

"You're a cold-blooded little bastard, aren't you?" he asked me, breathing hard. He meant the words to sting but it was just another emotional cloudburst, a break in the weather. In a minute he would go on to something else, and he did. "I'm sorry," he said. "Every time they call about Ellen it seems to get worse."

"I know," I said. "We should get going."

This made him angry again, but anything I said would have made him angry. I'd learned long before this not to get my hopes up. Inside my father, at least when he was drunk, I pictured a multicolored mess, like a spin-art picture, bright colors spilling everywhere. I just wanted to go. Shaking his head sadly at me, disappointed, he crawled into the backseat of the Plymouth and sat straight up on the hump in the middle of the backseat, blocking the whole rear-view mirror.

It was eleven o'clock by then, or eleven-thirty. The greasy kids from my high school were driving up and down King's Boulevard in their cars, engine noises and screaming, the sound of breaking glass, while we lumbered toward the interstate in the Plymouth. This car was everything my father believed himself to be and was not: it was safe, it was slow, it was green, it was square, it was as reliable as a cinder block and about as fast. It had four doors, an AM-only radio and an aftermarket air conditioner that you banged your knees against. Advantages: dependability, good gas mileage and a backseat wide enough for making out, on the beach or parked in the palmetto scrub, soft Florida nights. And this car was invisible to cops, or should have been—my father had gotten his third DWI the year before, and now had to take the bus to work, and drink within walking distance. I never had any trouble with the car, not in high school, or for a long time after. The way that things go on seems remarkable to me. Children are born, parents die, marriages start and bloom and begin to fade and still the Plymouth runs along, needing only a set of tires sometimes, or a voltage regulator.

My father was asleep by the time we got to 95, a bag of laundry with a necktie on, slumped across the backseat, where I'd been almost-fucking with Penny Silvers the weekend before. I stopped at a gas station at the edge of the city sprawl, filled the tank and bought a twenty-four-ounce coffee, then eased back into the stream of northbound trucks, driving limousine-careful so I wouldn't wake him. This was one of those summer nights that seemed as full of possibility as the day. I eased the window down slowly, carefully, and let the damp wind fill the car, and this trip began to seem almost like a pleasure cruise, an escape from a dull summer. I couldn't completely forget what was in front of us, but I was able to put it off to the side; I had money in my pocket, a full tank of gas and Georgia stretched out in front of me. A hundred miles into the trip, I didn't know how far I'd gone or how far I had left to go. I was easy in the driver's seat, relaxed, enjoying the night air and the rock and roll from the beach-town radio stations I was able to pick up.

As we passed Savannah the road turned inland, and then for some reason I started to remember. A few hours from now, maybe even the next morning, we would see her and she would ask us why we had left her. The question was for me. She could understand my father's deserting her, he wasn't strong himself, but I was her son. And this was true and it was always true and I couldn't deny it. She was always my mother, always recognized me and reached for me, even when she was so filled with rage or fear that she didn't seem capable of holding anything else. I wanted to say, she's not herself, like the other visitors in the wards. But it was never true. She was always herself, always mine, always my mother. And I'd tried to deny her. I tasted ashes in my mouth, following my headlights north, the red and yellow marker-lights of the lumbering trucks. The thought of seeing her the next day brought ashes to my mouth; the sight of my father, inert in the backseat, brought ashes to my mouth; the memory of Penny Silvers, the stupidity of trying to escape from the only life I was ever going to have.

Somewhere in South Carolina I stopped for gas, a lonely station in the middle of nowhere. The prices were bad but it wasn't my money. I checked the oil, paid the kid behind the counter and pulled the car around to the side. In the bathroom I splashed water on my face, stared at my face in the mirror. When I came outside again, my father wasn't in the car.

I saw him through the window of the gas station, pulling at the doors of the beer coolers inside—but it was after two, they were locked, and the kid told him so.

"What the hell," my father said. I could hear him through the open door. He was in worse shape now than he'd been when he went to sleep, which happened sometimes. I don't know if it was the last drinks catching up to him, or if it was the sleep that confused him. He looked like a drunk in a TV comedy, like Johnny Carson playing drunk, reeling around the aisles, yelling at the kid. "There isn't anybody around to see you," he said. "Come on! All I want is a damn six-pack."

The kid was my age or a little older, a skinny, nervous-looking guy with bad zits. One of those country kids, he'd never been anywhere. "We can't sell no beer after two," he said. "That's a state law."

"All I want is a damn beer," my father said. "Just open up the damn cooler for a minute and sell me a damn beer, all right? OK?"

As he stumbled toward the counter, I saw the boy's hand go down and take hold of something—a baseball bat, maybe, or a tire iron, but it looked like a gun to me, just from the way he was holding it. "Dad!" I yelled out, but he didn't hear me. I couldn't move, I could only watch.

9

"It's a state law," the kid said.

"Just open the cooler, OK? That's all I want."

My father's voice was tired and easygoing now, but he kept walking, slowly shuffling toward the counter, and I saw the kid's hand tighten, the tendons in his wrist standing out like wires.

"Look, you get out," he said, but my father didn't seem to notice. Now, I thought, it's going to happen now. And I was locked into my place, just watching. I couldn't seem to move. I closed my eyes and in my imagination I saw the kid raise the gun, the shots, blood spattering, and I thought, Go on, go ahead and pull the trigger.

I waited to hear the sound of the gunshots but nothing came.

When I opened my eyes a moment later, my father had stopped. "I don't know what kind of damn place this is," he said. He stood there a moment longer, then left the store, went out to the car, sat upright in the backseat. The kid came to the window and looked at my father. He saw me out there in the dark and I wanted to hide from his eyes. I was ashamed for myself, not for my father. After a minute the kid went back to his counter and my father lay down again in the backseat.

I could hear crickets everywhere around me in the dark.

I walked out into an empty field next to the station, with my heart still beating fast. Big interstate trucks roared by on the highway, which was up on an embankment, twenty or thirty feet above my head. Their headlights threw my shadow out in front of me in the dirt, a long thin shape of a man racing around in a half-circle as the trucks passed by and then lost in the darkness, to form again as another pair of headlights passed. I had money in my pocket and a suitcase full of clothes. One of the trucks would stop for me, sooner or later. I thought of all the places I could be by the next day: Key West or New York City or Chicago, heading west.

It wasn't so much that I wanted somebody to kill him, I didn't care if he was dead or not. I just wanted that weight off of me. I stood there watching my shadow circling around in the headlights and thinking about Wyoming, a place where I had only been to once, the summer before. I was hitching out to Seattle and I got a ride all the way to Wyoming from a girl named Karen. I still had her address in my wallet, frayed and faded to almost nothing. It wasn't boyfriend-girlfriend or anything, we just got along. I always thought I had a friend in Wyoming, a place I could go to. All I had to do was step up onto the embankment and stick my thumb out. If I wanted to I could go back to the car first and get my clothes, maybe leave my father some gas money in his jacket pocket. He didn't have a license but he'd be OK to drive, once he slept through the night—unless the kid in the store decided to call the cops after all, or unless he decided to drive while he was still drunk, the way he did sometimes. Unless, unless, unless. There were all kinds of things that might happen.

I was just going to walk away. I was just going to let his life be his own. The next month, September, I would turn eighteen, which was old enough for anything.

In Wyoming, after the rain, the smell of the sagebrush is ten times as strong as before, like sagebrush perfume. I tried to imagine a sky full of Western stars, cold and distinct, instead of this mottled, milky Southern sky. Where I could be the next day: Kansas City, Cedar Rapids, New Orleans or Minneapolis, on the way to South Dakota, on the way to Wyoming. I looked at the trucks passing by on the highway again and I watched my shadow circle around me in the headlights, the thin man torn to nothing in the dark, again and again. After a few minutes of watching I turned back toward the car, where my father was sleeping.

dogs

LET'S SAY THINGS STOP WORKING OUT FOR YOU. LET'S SAY YOU run out of money in a city that doesn't know you, and the only job they find for you is killing dogs on the night shift. Your car dies. Your apartment is not quite far enough from the shelter.

That distant sound of barking dogs is amplified by your memory, by dreams, so that it fills your grainy, sleepless mornings, the way that barking fills the shelter like water, a thick, swirling weight of sound that makes it hard to move, that spills out of the shelter, that ebbs and subsides and then, one dog at a time, starts again. Every kind of sound, yipping shih tzus, baying coonhounds, Pomeranians and Dobermans and vocalizing mutts. Some of the dogs bark so long and loud that they lose their voices before you can kill them, they go out with puny squeaks, shaking their heads, wondering what's wrong. You give them a shot, pile them in the chamber, pump the air out. Then the incinerator.

The trees that you remember every morning in your dreams, midwestern oaks and elms and leafy poplars, are shrunk to bitter twigs here. The only green in this city carpets the cemeteries. The remaining life is draining down into the roots: half-empty old women wander the supermarkets, the libraries, pardon me, pardon me. The knuckles of old men. While the bodies of the dogs you kill are beautiful, especially the greyhounds: piled in the cart on their way to the incinerator, they look like sleeping ballerinas, waiting for Cinderella. They belong onstage. The racing dogs arrive on your shift, dozens of them, on the night that racing season is over for the year. You picture them under the lights, straining toward the artificial rabbit while the tourists scream their names.

You report at eleven, you kill the night's dogs at twelve, from two till four you hose down the cages, after four the shelter doesn't care what you do. Once a month the phone rings but it's a wrong number. Each dog has a little card posted on the outside of the cage, a card filled out by the owners:

Name, Breed, Sex, Weight, Spayed/Neutered, Shots, Reason. You read the Reasons and wonder who could ever pass this test: Not good w/ kids; Needs company; Moving to new apt. does not allow pets; Barks. You fill out cards on the owners and slip them into the card file at night, knowing that no one will ever look, tens of thousands of Names, of Reasons: Not good w/ animals.

The shelter uses these multiplying library cabinets as proof of its efficiency, but the names don't matter, just the number, the bulk of them. These empty hours before dawn, the shelter bursting with the voices of the reprieved, you review the accidents that brought you here, and the intentions. Let's say that your mother died young. You lost a picture of yourself. Some nights you bring a half-pint of Jim Beam to doctor the coffee.

There's a procedure for leaving a dog to be killed, you try to tell the girl, but she is just gone, tires smoking gravel out of the parking lot. The dog looks through you, frantic—a pretty little bitch, some sort of Border collie cross or Australian shepherd. Who will do the paperwork? You take out a card and begin to make things up: her name is Ginger, the girl that Gilligan never got. The bitch is two, more or less—you guess it from her teeth—and her owner was a college girl, so she's had her first shots but not the recent ones. Ginger's claws skitter on the linoleum floor, trying to follow the long-gone car. It's just light, quarter to five. When you get to the line for Reason you see the apparition of the college girl: bottle-blond, a little heavy, she drove some little American shitbox like a Chevette. Not one of the beautiful ones, the ones who couldn't lose. Her makeup was smeared in black profusion across her cheeks, as if she had been crying.

Think of a dog's loyalty, the weight of that uncomplicated love. You remember minutes after you first made love, staring out the window of a girl's suburban bedroom at the dirty snow in her yard, the dark bones of the trees, and wondering how you would stand up under the weight of love that had been entrusted to you, the promises you meant to keep—promises that meant everything to you, though not as much to her. Later this gets mixed up with the barking, but the idea of snow, of virginity, starts tears in your chest. You reach down, unclip the leash from Ginger's collar and hold the door for her to go, running, racing toward the college girl with all the grace of her beautiful dog's body.

Even if she finds her owner, she'll be back. And there are other futures: delivery trucks and dogcatchers, kids with .22s down in the wash, shooting rusty appliances, anything that moves. But still. The dogs in the cages behind you bark furiously, angry and begging, wanting only the chance that Ginger got: to be released into the wide and loveless world to find their owners. Let's say you retreat into the chain-link pens, where tomorrow's dead dogs race and whimper, frantic for love, barking and barking. And you have the keys to every lock, the means to open the cages, open the doors and send them racing. You'll be a hero, king of the dogs. Strangers will know your name in the world of dogs.

But in the world of men, the dogs will continue to be killed. You can be replaced, easily. You can be replaced. The morning traffic has started, the morning cars on their way to work, the big machine awakening, moving forward, spitting out junk, broken parts, dead dogs, junk. The nonstop barking drives the last thought from your mind. Quite suddenly you hate the dogs, all of them. You put the keys back in your pocket. Their barking is injuring you. You stand in the sunlight, feeling the yellow warmth of morning on your useless body.

pretty judy

JUDY'S WINDOW WAS NEAR THE TOP OF THE HOUSE, NEXT TO THE supple tip of a tall, straight juniper tree, she'd lean out and call to the schoolchildren as they passed by, in the morning and again in the afternoon, especially the boys. A white house with green shutters in a lake of brilliant lawn, a tulip tree spreading over the grass and flowers and hedges, the pair of candle-shaped junipers guarding the chimney all the way up to the third story, all rambling, graceful, not too perfect. Her mother, Mrs. MacGregor, coached her at the beginning of every school year, so that by October Judy knew nearly everyone's name. October mornings, the rain splattering out of the leaves of the trees that lined the streets, their limbs meeting overhead, a tunnel of green turning gold, and Judy's high clear voice drifting down: Hi Jerry! Hi Mary! Hi Paul!

But school was out, this was June, another rainy month, but more optimistic. Paul was coming back alone from the high school courts, where he'd hit a yellow tennis ball against the backstop for forty-five minutes. He said to himself, I am solitary, I am not lonely. My mother is a pediatrician, my father is an architect, I am going to college. Still, it was sweet to hear the high, piping voice float down from her window: Hi Paul! Hi Paul!

Hi Judy!

Come say hi to me!

OK! he said, and walked up onto the lawn. Hi Judy!

You couldn't tell what was wrong with Judy by looking at her face, except that she would forget sometimes to close her mouth, and easy questions would worry her. Everything she felt was on her face, now round as a cartoon sun, pleased, elbows on the sill, staring down at him. The neighborhood said she was nineteen, or even twenty-one, but really she was a kid, kid T-shirts, lollipop colors, big and pink, glossy blond hair cropped blunt at her neck. All day, in the summer emptiness, the familiar streets and sidewalks had felt strange to Paul; he was fifteen, growing out of his boy's body into something else; he had passed her house a thousand times and still knew nothing about her. What was it like in Judy's room?

In the driveway was a greasy spot where Judy's mother's station wagon was not.

Can I come in?

Come in, yes! Come say hi to me!

Curiosity wasn't all of it. He crept around to the kitchen door like a thief, though this was the proper door—in this neighborhood the front door was for company, the side or back for familiars. He prayed this was not the day for the cleaning woman. The neighborhood boys told rumors about Judy, and Paul did not want to be misunderstood, or understood at all; he wanted to be alone, weightless, he wanted this to be happening in his imagination. The halls of the MacGregors' house were mournful, serious, other people's dead peering down at him from smoky paintings. The stairs were light maple, like a bowling alley, but the banister was some dark wood, deep red, like dried, polished blood. He was still holding his tennis racket, a ticket of membership. Red carpets with dark patterns, baskets of dried grasses and leaves, neat and tidy, scented with wax and lemons. Their other children were away at college. Paul guessed wrong on the third floor, opened the wrong door —to the attic, bare wood and piles of old *New Yorkers* and clothes—and again he felt that his life and everything in it was just a sham, something put up quickly for the sake of a picture, the thickness of a photograph.

Paul, she said, Pauletta Paulotta Paulola Pauleeleelu.

Standing plainly in the middle of the carpet, as if she wasn't sure what to do with her body, too big to hide.

How are you, Judy?

I was watching, she said. I always am.

Mournful deep green plaids on the cushions in the window seat, the rocking chair, the flounced bed; Paul had been expecting dolls, primary yellows. And she was big. She always surprised everyone at picnics or at the annual yard sale, Paul's height at least, and imposing. Not fat but big, with tiny feet— how could her feet support her? She was a familiar face, but apart from her face he knew nothing about her. He had never been alone with her before, nor in her room, and he did not know what he was doing there; he was nervous, waiting to leave, wanting to stay. He did not know where to stand. Windows open, a rainy trickle of air filtering through the trees. Paul looked down at the sidewalk, an empty place, waiting.

A car, Judy said. There's one. Make it go.

Go where?

I was playing with the cars, she said. I think that if I think, I can make them go faster or slow down or go the same, or maybe I don't. I don't know.

I'll make it go left, he said, and they both watched. The car went straight, tires swishing on the wet pavement. It had started to rain again. What was he supposed to say? Something. Beyond her familiar shape she was so unknown. A slight voltage of alarm.

That's nice, he said.

Judy looked at him, frowned. He was making her un-
happy. Someday the perfect playmate, but it wouldn't be him.
He could think of nothing that would make her better. They
knelt together on the window-seat cushion, touching at the
shoulder and the hip, a shared rainy sadness, neither of them
was right. Gradually Paul became aware of her body, her
warmth and weight. What would she allow him? A red Volvo
passed under the window, a black sedan. His hand reached
out, he watched it like a movie, and touched her bare forearm
below the sleeve of her sweatshirt. Paul himself didn't touch
her, only his hand.

Oh, Judy said.

Paul felt his heart start in his chest like a big rough motor,
wondered what he had done. The sound of her voice, her little
cry, was like nothing he had heard from a human voice, pure
pleasure, he thought, she must have very sensitive skin. He
touched her bare neck and saw her head wave blindly back and
forth, eyes closed, like a dreamer seeing a beautiful city in the
distance.

Oh, she said again, and Oh! as he touched her breast
through the layers of fabric, sweatshirt and brassiere, remembering that the world could see them through her window,
tugging her down to the carpeted floor, out of sight. She followed him obediently, it seemed to Paul that she was blind to
anything but touch, drunk with it. He lifted her sweatshirt and
then put his hand on the hard lace of her brassiere, no resis-

tance, only her soft, lost voice, he rolled her onto her side, reached behind her and fumbled with the little hooks until by some miracle her bra came unsprung and her big soft breasts tumbled against him. Paul felt drunk himself, with excitement and with panic. He had fumbled in playrooms before, in cars and in the rough grass of the neighborhood parks, girls from the neighborhood who would negotiate a touch, or on some lucky Saturday allow his blind hand to wander in the darkness of their jeans, but this, this plain revelation, was new to him. She wouldn't stop him, wouldn't stop him from anything, her hunger for every new touch was so direct. He knew what he was risking, the air itself was lit with danger, knew that if either of them was going to stop this, it would not be her, but she was so close, so open to him.

Paul had one last lucid moment, sitting away to undo his belt, her sweatpants lying beside her and her shirt hiked around her shoulders, the defenseless bulk of Judy. "Oh," she said again and again, as if this moment's absence of his hands were more than she could bear; and Paul saw what he was doing, knew that it was wrong, he meant to apologize and to leave, yet there she was, he could not stop looking. He didn't, he remembered later, bother to fasten his belt again, but there wasn't any Judy anymore, only this: a pink, mewling thing, cries that started back in her throat, as if he were hurting her, the last trace of language gone. Her little hands were callused, hard as a carpenter's. Later he would think of her in animal terms: she mewled like a kitten, bawled and bucked like a hungry calf, and still later—years after—he would decide that this was because there was so little human veneer to her; that sex and awareness were natural enemies, a battle every time between modesty, a sense of order and of embarrassment, and the little kindling flame of desire. But Judy's desire was pure, reservations, questions burnt away, an animal thing, he told himself, an animal thing, but he met her in it and matched her, lost in guilt, engulfed, unwilling to stop, to breathe. He couldn't seem to stop, he came as soon as he was inside her.

Don't stop, she said.

Paul's mouth had filled with sand, the whore, the horror. Pants around his knees, he slid shamefully from inside her and leaned against the window seat, a sickness quickly filling him that he would not be able to vomit out. Thoughts of escape.

Don't stop, she said again, turned her head toward Paul and briefly focused her eyes on him, then let them go blank again, turned her face to the wall, dropped her hand between her legs and quickly brought herself off again, cat-cries that the whole world could hear, listening from the window. Then said something he didn't catch.

What's that? he asked, dragging the words from somewhere inside.

Pretty Judy, she whispered to the wall.

Then he knew what she was asking for, and for a moment he thought that he would just leave, disappear. But some reserve of courage found him, and he reached out a reluctant hand and whispered, That's right. Pretty Judy.

Pretty Judy, she said.

He stroked the soft curve of her hip, her fascination hadn't left him, even in his shame. Pretty Judy, he said.

The slam of a car door jolted him upright, he went to the window and peered carefully through but it wasn't Mrs. Mac-Gregor, not yet. The neighbors. But still.

She turned her face from the wall, like a dreamer, still half in sleep. You better go, she said. I don't want my mom to get mad.

Paul heard this like a reprieve. He gathered his clothes back into order, looked back from the doorway, but she didn't seem to expect a kiss, still lying pink, inert, half-naked. And he didn't want to kiss her then. Had he at all? Yes, he remembered her busy, surprising tongue in his mouth. Demons of shame whipped him down the stairs, out into the clean, rain-washed streets and down the sidewalk, as if all this had happened in a sidewalk crack, an excursion out of time, a moment of imagination.

Hi Paul!

He tensed, heart in his throat, as if the trees and air had announced him guilty for all the neighborhood to hear. Looked up, saw her waving, back in her sweatshirt. Paul waved unsurely, turned his back on her, walked away, felt her eyes on his neck until he reached the cover of the sheltering trees. Walking away, betrayal. Closing his eyes, feeling her heavy breasts against him, he nearly tripped over one of the Morganfield kids rounding the driveway on a Big Wheel.

Hey, fuck you, the kid said.

Paul grinned. Fuck you, too, he said. A kid again for a moment, biggest kid on the block, he could get his way, but then he tripped over the word fuck, and remembered. He walked on toward his house and he knew, stood convicted: he was like her, they were equal. Not then, but in that green bedroom, two bodies, neither better than the other. This was the worst thing to know about himself: he was just like her, they were equal. He saw her busy hand between her legs, blank eyes, and thought of all the times in the shower or in his room.

This awful equality frightened him, worse than the guilt. He was just like her, and he tried to defend himself as he walked toward his house: her fault, but it wasn't, he knew it; only curiosity, but he knew the rumors before he went, he couldn't deny it. He could have stopped, anytime, he'd known. It seemed like somebody else, in memory, it had never happened.

It had never happened, as long as it was a secret, who would Judy talk to, who would Judy tell? He imagined her mouth rounding around the words I fucked Paul, and her mother's straight mouth and iron hair, a tidy, self-sacrificing fifty. Plaid skirts, church on Sunday. If she found out she would put him in jail, and that would be easy; better than this, this black, corrosive secret, cancer of the mind. But Judy would never tell, and Paul would never tell. He dragged his secret, like the body of a dead dog, up the back steps to his kitchen, where his mother, the pediatrician, was making tuna salad in the skylit brightness.

Hi sweetie, she said. Where's your tennis racket?

Paul lit like a man on a hot wire. He didn't have an answer for this, and his mother looked at him curiously, seeing right through his pants and his shorts to his wet, guilty dick. I loaned it to Colin, he finally said.

I thought he was in Denver.

Denmark, Paul said. He's coming home tomorrow.

Both of them took a moment to realize this made no sense. Paul added, I put it in his garage, as if this would make anything clear. He felt his hands grow until they were enormous bald red things, guilty secrets that would not be concealed, then realized he'd have to go on the offensive if he was going to escape.

He said, I don't know, I guess I'm having sort of a hard time.

His mother's handsome face darkened with concern. She was a fan of emotional honesty, she thought it was healthy, a guarantee of a good childhood, her specialty. Although he would have to think of something to tell her later.

Paul said, Can we talk later? Right now I just want to think some things through. I'm basically OK. OK?

OK, his mother said, little furrows of concern rising at the inner edges of her eyebrows. She waved her chef's knife helplessly in the air as he retreated to his room, not one o'clock yet, watery afternoon light, the afternoon and the evening to be gotten through before there was any prospect of sleep, and sleep was all he wanted, the black invisibility. Paul wanted to become invisible to himself, he seemed like evidence. Thinking of his tennis racket, ticking like a terrorist's dream in Judy's room, thinking, I will be punished for this. The discovery, trial by disappointment, maybe worse.

Whatever, he thought. Anything he could touch would be easier than this. Anything outside himself. Jimi Hendrix stared down at him from the wall, psychedelic purple and green, a dirty mouth under a thin, sinister mustache. Paul took his purple Telecaster from its case in the closet, a better guitar than he should have had but money was not a problem in this house.

He plugged it into a Tube Screamer and then into a headphone amp and turned the distortion up to ten and played his same stupid chords and clumsy leads. He was never better, never even good, but it passed the time, he could lose himself completely, a closed loop, fingers to guitar to amp to ears, no one else to hear him, like jacking off. Hendrix's eyes, eyes that could look at anything. The afternoon disappeared, a pencil line under an eraser. He played until his fingers hurt, and then till one of them bled a little.

Paul put his guitar away as the light was leaving the windows, no lamps yet, a gray, ghostly light, and from behind the pile of records at the back of his closet he took a tattered *Penthouse,* and opened it to a photograph of two girls faking sex with each other, ghostly girls in the half-light, secret skin in tight close-up, and Paul knew, looking at the picture, that he had thought of nothing else all afternoon: tongue in his mouth, animal voice in his ear, hard little carpenter's hands.

I will be good, he told himself, no idea what he meant.

That night he dreamt of her, woke up hard in the darkness of his room, a room that was newly strange, images of birds, of houses seen from a great height, persisting from some earlier part of his dream. A stranger to himself, an unsolvable problem, if train A leaves city X at five-thirty and travels north, he wandered the dark hallways toward the kitchen, hoping for ice cream. He'd barely eaten at dinner. Even his father had noticed.

———

Summer, school was out, his few friends had left town, nothing days. His mother sat with him after breakfast, inquired about drugs, he was scheduled to start a job in three weeks, did he need something to fill the time? Anomie, he said, bringing a smile to her face with the new word, the one thing he did right all day. The tennis racket ticked in a corner of Judy's room, without going off. Tuesday nothing Wednesday nothing Thursday nothing, but he prowled the streets, a thief of opportunity, telling himself that he was only going to get the racket back. His nights were populated with versions of Judy, *Penthouse* dolls, secret skin, not the child who called to him still, Hi Paul! when he walked by to see if Mrs. MacGregor's car was in the driveway—it always was—or the cleaning woman was there, but the tongue in his mouth, cries in his ear. He could not connect the two, could not believe that the afternoon had been anything but a dream, though now it was his everyday life that seemed like a dream, nothing weighed anything, nothing mattered, he found himself trying to read the clouds. It continued to rain, never hard, never letting up. Judy was growing inside him like a child, taking shape, stretching to be born, feeding on his blood. Even his father noticed.

He was only going to get the racket back. Friday morning he saw Mrs. MacGregor's car swish by under the arching trees, a flash of imitation woodgrain, a chance. A man two streets over had built a speedboat in his basement, a beautiful shape of varnished, steam-bent maple, without thinking how he was going to get it out. This was twenty years before, the house had been sold twice, the boat was still there.

———

Paul, she said, Pauletta Paulotta Paulola Pauleeleelu.

There in the corner was the tennis racket, and there she was. The air was turning fire-engine green, a whining in his ears like television, he wanted to lie down on the floor and cry like a baby boy.

She said, My mom is gone all day.

He lay down on the floor. Without affection, she came and lay beside him. The carpet was thick, soft and green, like a lawn, and as her clumsy fingers fumbled with his pants Paul wondered what the name for this was, fucking seemed too hard, making love seemed preposterous, maybe, as he lost the name for anything, maybe that was part of it, no name because it wasn't anything human. Paul gave up his thoughts, met Judy on the carpet as body to body, equals, he remembered, equals. As he gave himself over to her hard little hands, he realized that only the things around it were at all human: courtship and roses, satin, magazines, going steady, we only owned the box, the thing in the box belonged to someone else, before words; and words extinguished themselves in his brain, though his eye kept recording, memories like pictures, her face, which was like an empty house, the rain in the trees outside, the plaid bedspread. Better than anything, but he wondered, in the shocked quiet afterward, what he was letting himself in for. He didn't know anything.

She said, I want some ice cream, Paul. Get me some, please.

Left her lying on her side, her back to him, like an accident victim, heavy and inert. Nearly left, when he got to the kitchen, but remembered that his racket was still upstairs—the first joke, first hint that he was being played with. He thought of Judy and her cars, go left, now stop, and wondered who or

31

what was watching him. Ice cream, two spoons, back along the morose hallways. What would it be like? A mommy, a daddy, a house. The ghostliness of these recent days came over him again, and he imagined that he would one day have all this, a house as big and fine as this one, a wife like Judy, only more intelligent, like looking down a deep hole into the future. A wife like Judy, what was so different? What was so wrong? But he knew as soon as he saw her, dressed again, big and drooping. They sat in the window seat and finished the ice cream, and when another kid walked by, Paul ducked out of sight and watched her lean out the window and wave, stretching her limbs eagerly like a plant bending toward the sun, and her smile and her sweet voice, Hi Larry! and the happiness that came and left her face so quickly, like breath on a mirror.

She seemed disappointed when her eyes turned into the room again and found him still there. Too much to think about. He pulled her down to the floor again.

Then a weekend at the beach with Mom and Dad, a relief in a way, he hoped things would become clearer, or go away. For the first time Paul was afraid of himself, what he was capable of. He thought of Judy in dirty particulars, every waking minute, he couldn't stop, he wanted air. He sat in the breakfast nook talking about the design of kites with his father, at the same time swearing to himself that he would never walk down her block, at the same time starring in his pornographic memories. He lay in the dunes alone, a hollow pocket of sand rimmed with saw grass, out of the wind, feeling the warm, cleansing sun pour down on his skin, and the whole world seemed to turn into Judy: Judy in the softness of the sand, in the warmth of the sun, in the ebb and tickle of the wave's retreat, especially Judy in the way the sand retreated from under his feet in the outwash, left him standing uneven, unsure of even the ground.

He swore that he would never see her again, never closer than the sidewalk, but this was not the truth. He decided that the kindest thing to do would be to be friends, like regular people. He dreamt about putting his hand between her legs, and it was always her. In practical terms he watched a lot of television, played his guitar, took solitary walks. It seemed impossible for his parents to know nothing, he was wearing her on every inch of his skin, but they were too caught up in their own romance, getting to know each other again was how they put it. They seemed like children to Paul, willful, self-absorbed children.

He stole a chance to see her on Monday, she was glad to see him and he was so pleased to see her smile that he wondered if he were in love. More words for something that there weren't any words for, he was learning. No time for anything that day, though, he had to slip out over the roof to avoid the cleaning lady. A near miss, he was taking chances. He felt tainted but he knew he couldn't turn away from her. Friday was her day alone, he knew, her mother went to volunteer at the Anglican Senior Citizens' Day Care Center, her father worked, the cleaning lady disappeared back into the dark reaches of the invisible city. How would he live till Friday? He would not see her Friday, he made up his mind again and again. He was definite on this point.

Then the miracle: Mrs. MacGregor drove away at ten Wednesday morning, leaving Judy undefended in the house. Paul saw the station wagon from the window of his room, and knew as it turned the corner, went away, that it didn't matter what he thought, he was going. He stayed in his room for another half an hour, but it was futile, the only idea that presented itself was that it didn't matter, right or wrong, crazy or real, he was going. His will seemed to count for nothing at all. I will treat her with compassion, he declared to himself, like the human being that she is. This sounded like the Boy Scouts, even to his own ears: when he closed his eyes, trying to think, he saw her blank-eyed shiver at the touch of his fingertips. Sleepwalking, dreaming his hand in front of his face. He was wrong, he was born wrong, he was broken.

Judy, he said, is your mother gone?

She nodded.

All day?

All day, she said happily, just like a child, just like the child she really was. Mom said to get my lunch on the table.

I want to take you to the zoo, he said, surprising himself with a sudden rush of moral correctness. Go see the animals, the bears and the giraffes and the elephants. Do you want to?

No, I want to do it. I want you to do it.

We can do it later, don't you want to go?

She looked at him, the window, the carpeted floor. OK, she finally said, still reluctant. He was just starting to realize how much time she spent in a bad mood.

He asked, Are those the clothes you want to wear?

But she didn't know, too complicated a question, and so he let it drop, wondering if her mother dressed her still: a pink sweatshirt with a big yellow sun on it, blue sweatpants, Keds. Big sunny Judy. They could just stay, Paul knew it, the thought of all that tangible skin, the slippery, solid bulk of her beneath him, a thickness of cloth away from his empty hands, but he was going to be right today.

Out the back door, then, through the alley as quickly as he could drag her along, the terror of discovery behind every fence. Even on the avenue, he kept his eyes fixed straight ahead, magic vision, if he couldn't see anyone then they couldn't see him, or sun-bright Judy either, waiting docile and obedient next to him in the bus shelter. He started to breathe again on the bus, the happy couple, Judy looking neat and nearly pretty on the seat beside him; and she was pretty to Paul, despite her size, he could touch her anywhere in memory and she seemed to him so much softer and enclosing than any normal girl could ever be. They rode across town without talking, watching the streets; and Paul felt that she could be anyone, that nothing was really so wrong, that they were different but other couples were different, too. The comfort of her nearness, her side pressed to his; but when they went through the poor part of town, deserted streets bright with advertising, a car on fire down one of the side streets surrounded by a village of flashing police cars, he remembered what a dangerous place the city was; a moment's worry, memory of things that hadn't happened yet.

The zoo was empty, the bears asleep, the giraffes staring thoughtfully as they ate, evaluating the flavor of every eucalyptus leaf. Paul felt the weight of how much he knew: elephant, sycamore, the distance to the stars, how to check the oil in his father's car, how to pay for things, her blank uncomprehending stare at the ticket booth, not even caring: beyond her. Yet her company was right for this place, she saw the strength of the tiger, ignored the path he had worn in the grass. The sadness of the rhinoceri, lying sideways in the mud like wrecked trucks, the manic intensity of the monkeys' stare and the bare patches on their skin where they had picked away each other's fur, all this eluded her; and she ran from cage to cage, laughing, delighted when anything moved. Her hair, glossy and fair as a blond child's, shined in the scattered sunlight, and her face in happiness was nearly pretty.

At first Paul liked her company, her cheerfulness, young and strong in the sun, delightful things to see, the promise of ice cream later. Gradually, though, he began to lose heart, there was too much she didn't see, and the other patrons stared at her when she talked in her overloud voice, Look Paul, look Paulie, elephants! He wanted to flip them all off, wanted to be transported, back to Judy's room. In his black heart he knew he had betrayed both of them. He wasn't interested in her, or she in him; what held them together was sex and nothing more. He was angry with her; she should have known.

Suddenly she whirled to face him, fear and anger on her face. No! she screamed. No, Paulie!

What?

36

I don't want to, Paulie!

People were staring, he looked around and saw a straggling band of badly retarded adults staring down into the empty otter pen, the pool where they weren't, their keepers explaining.

I don't want to!

What?

Go with them! I don't want to!

You don't have to.

I want to go! she said. I don't want to stay here!

OK, he said, all right. He put it together as he led her toward the gate, she must have thought he meant to leave her here, or at least the fear. She stumbled, looking behind. The anger had passed from her face but the fear remained.

Ice cream, Paul said. You want some?

No! I want to go!

After we leave, he said. He had to calm her down somehow. Outside the gate she seemed less agitated, outside the bars, away from the cages. He led her past the duck pond, toward the derelict hot dog stand in faded red-and-white that stood across the pond from the entrance to the zoo. The morning sun was getting hot, Judy was tiring, so he had to drag her a little to get her to come along with him, but she brightened when she saw the boats, little paddleboats that seated two, which one pedaled like a bicycle.

Boats, Paulie! Judy shouted.

Don't you want some ice cream?

I want to go in the boats.

He knew then what a bad idea this trip had been. He was getting hot himself, and the prospect of paddling around this duck-fouled acre of water, exposed to the hot sun and fully visible to any passer-by, did not please him. But there was no way around it. He paid the candy-striped boy behind the iron grille and took command of boat 17, an aqua plastic double bathtub, settled her into the sun-hot seat and pushed away. Again he saw the maimed and crippled ducks, their senseless fights, their shit fermenting on the concrete shore, while Judy, in the purity of her delight, saw only the sparkling sun on the water, the happy trees, the smiling clouds and the happy little boat. The sun embroidered on her sweatshirt, it felt like he was carrying a suitcase full of someone else's things. He began to feel a headache.

Three times around the little willow-draped island in the center of the pond, always in the same direction because Judy couldn't get the drift of paddling, they always went left. This tired him out, and he stopped, though he didn't want to. Judy looked to the left and to the right, and then she took his hand in her own hard little palm, led it to her bare forearm and sighed as she felt the soft pressure of his fingertips on her own sun-warm arm.

Oh, she said in drowsy delight.

For some reason this repelled him. We can't, he said, not here.

Just touch me.

Not here.

I want to go home, she said.

OK, Paul said, relieved. Let me put the boat away.

No, I want to go home.

We have to put the boat away.

Mom! she cried. I want my mom!

Abruptly she stood up, nearly tipping the little tub over, and looked around the shore, expecting to see her mother.

Mom! she cried out. Mom! Mom!

A silence spread along the dirty shores of the pond, and every stranger's face was turned toward them. He took her hand, tried to coax her down onto the seat again, but she shook free, and he could not move the boat with her standing up. Twice she nearly fell into the water, and then he gave up, closed his eyes and hoped for whatever there was to hope for, which was nothing, nothing he could think of. The sun was pleasant, though, and the sound of the water lapping against the fiberglass hull, little hollow drumming notes, like a marimba.

Mom! Judy yelled. Mom!

She was nearly crying, baffled, near the end of her rope. Heavy, flustered. He wondered what would happen next, wondered, if he never opened his eyes, if this could still be imaginary. Then heard the sound of an outboard motor start and stop and start again. He followed Judy's gaze: a tin Sears boat with three uniforms in it, the candy-striped kid from the ticket stand riding the motor, a park policeman sitting nervously in the middle, gripping the rim of the boat, and in the prow, standing, a zoo guard in his red uniform, one foot propped on the seat, smoking, looking like an admiral in the Italian navy, gold braid and a peculiar hat, and he was leaning forward, elbows on his raised knee, and staring at Judy and at Paul, and only then, at that moment, as he watched the zoo policeman take one last drag from his cigarette, then hurl the butt into the rushing, tea-colored water, did Paul realize how badly this was all going to end.

the victim

TELEPHONE SERVICE

TETHERED TO HER STATION BY A COIL OF BEIGE PLASTIC, A TINY
microphone in her mouth, voices in her ears, she feels her body

become part of the machine after the first few minutes of work, the type of work machines do better anyway: "Reservations this is Tina how can I help you?"

The clock starts running as soon as she picks up the call, a minute forty-five seconds to service them and on to the next, and the next, and so on. The machine kicks out her average at the end of every working day: she's been running slow, one-forty-eight, one-fifty-one. Mr. Beveridge (the human face of the machine, friendly and round, Tina suspects he might be gay) has already apologized for noticing this. "What is it?" he asked her. "Is something wrong? You've always been our champion."

Tina tries to think of what she might say, massaging her sore wrists.

THE TATTOO

An eagle, wings outstretched over his biceps, with a writhing snake caught in its talons. The tail of the snake winds around his arm and down to the soft veins inside his elbow. The colors are vivid, reds and greens, he's had it only a few months. Tina knows (watching him play bass with his awful little band, sweating on the black stage in a black sleeveless T-shirt) that if he lives long enough Bobby's tattoo will turn blue and fade and look as awful as the rest of them, all the old-man-blue tattoos slumped across the wattled skin of retired sailors and marines and cops.

But this prospect of age doesn't seem, to Tina, worth worrying about. She can't imagine him any way but young, as if on some future not-too-distant birthday his skin will split wide open and some new species of Bobby will emerge, a different animal entirely.

THE DOCTOR

Lacing her forearms into the canvas braces, he says, "These have to be tight for them to work."

"You want me to wear these everywhere?"

"Everywhere."

With a soft satisfied grunt, he ties her right arm snug into the brace, tan canvas reinforced with a hidden metal strap that runs along the inside of her arm from her elbow to her palm. They lace along the back, long tidy stitches like the laces of boxer's boots. When he's finished with both, Tina stands up, holding her arms before her. Her arms are rigid in their new jackets, stiff as weapons, too large for her body. The braces hold her palms open, tilt her wrists slightly back, so that she holds her hands toward the doctor like Jesus, vulnerable, welcoming (she thinks of the suffering bloody hands and the blank face of Jesus in her childhood church, the wounds that were so much more expressive than the mouth, the eyes).

"I wear these everywhere," she says again. "Even to work."

"I'm telling them at work to give you a break for a week or so. Come back on Tuesday, we'll do some range-of-motion tests, then we'll see."

"See what?"

"If you ought to go back to work or not," he says, and grins to himself; some wry private moment. "I know you love your job," he says.

43

HER BODY

When she sees it accidentally, changing clothes or bathing, her body looks pale, soft, arbitrary. But more than anything else, it looks *white*—blank as paper, an empty space to fill in.

She's scribbled on this emptiness herself: eleven earrings in her left ear, two in her right. She's shaved her legs and dyed her hair (blond and now black), dressed in leather and poured herself full of junk and sugar and Bobby's cheap vodka, trying to write a new version of herself—I am sexy, I am daring—but under the clothes is always this blank place, this absence, like the blank white bark of a paper birch into which boys carve their initials.

BLACK OVERCOATS

Black, boiling into gray froth as it pounds onto the beach, the ocean heaves and roars. An intermittent moon glitters between the slow-moving clouds. Somewhere out in the night, Tina knows, the darkness of the water must meet the darkness of the sky, and if she holds her head level enough she imagines she can see it: the thin, immaculate black line of the horizon. "Bobby," she says. "Bobby, I want to go home."

"What's wrong, baby?"

"I'm not kidding."

He seems to rouse himself, unfixes his eyes from the sea and grins at her. He says, "I didn't think you were kidding."

"It's too cold to swim."

"It's October," he says. "I could have told you. We didn't have to drive all the way over here to find out."

"I like driving with you."

"Tina," he says, "you're fucking nuts."

In their black overcoats they lean against a piling, soft sand under them. Bobby drinks from his pint, offers it to her, knowing she won't take it, then leans against her, taking her bound left hand into his pocket. A captive. His face is outlined in the slanting light that falls from the boardwalk lights above them, a drawing of a face. Feral, Tina thinks; the eyes of a Doberman. Though she knows it's an act.

HIS BODY

The physical body, interesting in itself: immaculately lean, he eats only grains and fruits, neither meat nor milk nor eggs nor fish, and he pedals his bicycle all day for a messenger service. His skin is thin, elastic, and his muscles ripple plainly under it as he moves. All that cycling has given him big, powerful legs; his hips are as full as a woman's but solid. His arms and his chest are less developed, not weak but thin. The way his pale torso rides on his heavy legs reminds her of a centaur, half-animal, half-warrior; she has seen these in museums, on the sides of ancient cups.

She sees something animal, too, something obscene in the way his neck supports his skull. He keeps his head nearly shaved, a black beard-stubble marking the outlines of where his hair might be, and through this shadow she can plainly see the muscles of his neck, the points where his tendons attach, his sinuous beating veins. She's rarely seen a naked head;

there's something still shocking about her first daily glance of him, even after these months together.

But what she remembers when he's gone isn't how he is but how he seems: solid, full of intention. He seems to fill his body completely, while Tina's managed to colonize only a tiny corner of her own. And when he's touching her, even just accidentally or casually (as the hand in the pocket tonight, his fingers wrapped around the taut canvas of the brace), she feels his intention spill out of him to fill the blank, amorphous mass of herself.

(Some nights she has to blur her eyes a little for this trick to work.)

CURLY FRIES, HOT DOGS, SKEE BALL, MISTER SOFTEE

Though the sidewalks are dark, deserted, and the shops all shut behind their metal grates, the blocks by the boardwalk keep their look of bright corruption. The cold salt breath of the ocean blows the signs back and forth: clowns, ice-cream cones, balloons. An audience of oversized stuffed animals perches behind the targets of the shooting gallery, imprisoned until spring, staring out through the metal bars at Tina and Bobby, who pass without noticing them.

THE ACCIDENT

A dark blue Monte Carlo sits awkwardly in a pool of street light, crumpled into the rear quarter of Bobby's beater Volvo.

(Two cars on the whole street, it's like a joke, something you'd find in a bubble-gum wrapper.) Bobby starts to run as soon as he sees it, but the Monte isn't going anywhere; the driver watches from behind the wheel as Bobby examines the damage. The driver waits for Tina to catch up before he gets out of his car. How long has he been sitting there?

"I'm fucking drunk," the driver says. "I'll tell you that right now. I'm sorry as shit about your car."

Bobby doesn't say a word, testing the bent metal of his car with little short kicks. Tina wonders what he's up to. The car is nothing to him, a two-hundred-dollar souvenir of his father's second marriage.

"Is this your car?" the drunk asks Bobby.

Bobby's still thinking, but she can't tell what. The night around them is loud with wind, an onshore breeze, as if the ocean didn't want any part of them, didn't even want to think about them. The drunk is wearing knife-pleated synthetic pants and a black cloth jacket with a lot of snaps and attachments, like the ones that pit crews wear at stock-car races, although to Tina he just registers as one word: asshole.

"I tell you," the drunk says. "That woke me right up. I was about falling asleep. Look, I can pay you for your car—let's just do this private, OK?"

"What do you mean?"

"I give you a couple of hundred bucks, you drive away, we don't tell anybody about it. I mean, if I've got to breathe into the tube, I'm going way downtown."

"What kind of money?"

"Like I say, a couple hundred bucks." He glances at the Volvo, missing hubcaps, torn seats (and in the moment of his glance Tina sees his contempt for the two of them, how it pains him to even talk). "I mean, I'm sorry, but we're not talking about a damn Mercedes or something."

"It's a foreign car," Bobby says.

"I could maybe go three hundred, three fifty. You'd best make up your mind, though—the cops show up, this deal won't make any difference to anybody."

"Shut the fuck up," Bobby says. "I didn't run into your car."

A mistake, Tina thinks: she sees the anger kindling in the eyes of the drunk, bright for a moment, then folding into their heavy lids, pretending to be sleepy. He folds his arms and leans heavily against the front fender of his car, which bows under his weight.

"All right then," the drunk says. "I guess we'll all just sit here and wait for the cops."

TINA CLOSES HER EYES

Pictures from her childhood: a tan stuffed horse; a picnic when she was small, when the grass in the park grew long and lush and green and her aunt teased her about how pretty she was becoming and the wind blew through the leaves of the tall eucalyptus trees, the air smelled like wet earth; a new white dress; a new tiny watch with a pink watchband.

A LIGHT, PRICKLING SWEAT

"Three-fifty?" Bobby asks. "Is that what we're talking about?"

The drunk smiles slowly. "I thought I said three hundred. I

don't know, man, I'm drunk. I'm liable to say damn near any-thing."

"You want to do this or not?"

"Course I do—wouldn't you want to stay out of jail if you could? It only makes sense."

Still he doesn't budge, rooted to the fender of the blue Chevrolet while the ocean wind blows through the streetlights and the telephone poles. He seems to be deciding something.

"Well, shit," he finally says. He turns to Tina. "You mind driving? I'm a little fucked up still."

"Where are we going?" she asks.

"Money's at my place. I don't carry that kind of cash with me, do you?"

Bobby says, "You didn't tell me you didn't have the money."

"I didn't say I didn't have it," the drunk says, grinning. "I said I didn't have it here. Either way, though, any way you want it."

Tina senses a sinister turn to this conversation: suddenly the drunk seems sly, in control. Tina thinks that she would rather be anywhere else than here (longing for the neutrality of work, of television, the empty, clean light of the supermarket).

"She can drive," Bobby says. "I'll follow you. How far away is it anyway?"

"Over the river and through the woods, to Grandmother's house we go," the sly drunk sings. "The horse knows the way to carry the sleigh through the white and drifting snow-o!"

"Shut the fuck up," Bobby says.

Tina sees the anger start into the drunk's eyes again, then quickly stored (for future reference, future use) as his eyes slide to half-mast again, as he thrusts a meaty hand toward

Bobby. "My name is Lyle," he says. "It's a pleasure to meet you."

LYLE

He slumps in the passenger seat, fat and regal, fumbling a Merit out of the crumpled pack on the dash. The inside of his car is like an ashtray with chairs.

OVER THE RIVER AND THROUGH THE WOODS

Tina eases the Monte Carlo into reverse and the cars uncouple. The metal of the bumpers grinds and squeals but Bobby's Volvo doesn't look any worse than before, really, and Lyle's car seems to be running fine, though one of the headlights is pointed up into the night. As they idle out of town with Bobby following, the crazy headlight hits the sensors on the street-light poles and they all switch off, so that a curtain of darkness follows behind them.

"About four miles out, straight down this road," Lyle says. "I'll show you before the turn. What'd you do there?" He aims his cigarette at her forearms in their braces.

"It's a work thing," Tina says. "Repetitive motion disorder."

(Between the big, important parts of the machine are wear zones, parts designed to absorb the vibration or the pounding of the engines. Without these cheap, replaceable parts, the big machines would have to take the punishment themselves. They would rattle themselves to bits. This is just the way things work, Tina knows, though it's strange to feel worn-out at twenty-four.)

"I thought it was something kinky," Lyle says, blinking at her bound wrists. "You look like you're capable of it."

Tina stiffens her grip on the wheel, startled out of her self-pity into a strange present.

"I mean that as a compliment," Lyle says.

The night is running by outside the windows of the car, beach pines and surprised-looking oaks in the glare of the crazy headlight. The yellow centerline runs under the car like Morse code: W-e h-a-v-e a m-e-s-s-a-g-e f-o-r T-i-n-a, W-e h-a-v-e a m-e-s-s-a-g-e f-o-r T-i-n-a, W-e h-a-v-e a m-e-s-s-a-g-e f-o-r T-i-n-a . . . *Take me away,* she replies, *get me out of here.* Bobby's Volvo seems like an island of safety, bobbing down the broken road behind them, connected by nothing more solid than the beams of his headlights. She longs to sit beside him on the taped-up seat. She imagines herself driving home at four in the morning while he sleeps beside her. The smell of the sea is all around them, soft muck of the tideflats and the stench of rotting clams.

Lyle leans toward her and traces a line with his finger from the base of her throat, between her breasts and down the center of her belly, stopping below her navel, letting his hand rest there. At first this seems unreal. She can't quite bring herself to reaction, and then it comes to her: that is his hand, this is my body.

"Get the fuck off me," Tina says.

Lyle complies, in no particular hurry. "I didn't think you'd mind," he says.

"Do you want me to stop the car?" She sounds like a substitute teacher, even to her own ears.

"Suit yourself," Lyle says, "but I don't think your boy-friend would be too happy about that, do you? We're talking about three hundred dollars here, three hundred dollars of my money."

He reaches for a cigarette but the pack is empty. When he opens the glove compartment for a fresh pack, Tina sees (or thinks she sees, in the dim light of the glove-box bulb, in the corner of her eye, in the moment before he slams the compart-ment shut again) a thing that scares her dry-mouthed and up-right, a bright blue electrical surge.

"He is your boyfriend, isn't he?" Lyle asks, fumbling with the cellophane. "Reason I ask is, he looks like a faggot, sort of."

"Just shut up, OK?"

"I'm just making conversation, to pass the time. I don't mean anything by it, you know, I don't have anything against faggots even. I just like to know where I stand."

"Please," Tina says, and she hears herself begging, and she knows he hears it, too. "Please, just for a minute, don't talk."

She can still feel, as if it were drawn in red paint or in blood, the line his finger traced down the center of her body.

She can still see, like a photograph printed on her retina, the bright silvery outline of the little gun she saw, or thought she saw, she can't be sure, next to the cigarettes in Lyle's glove compartment. "This is our turn here," Lyle announces. "Down this dirt road here. We're almost home."

SAFETY

Sometime in high school, Tina decided that her mother lived a life of fear, a search for protection from a dangerous world.

What she called "love" was only an inability to take care of herself. When she said to Tina "I love you, sweetheart," what Tina heard was "Help me, help me, help me."

Tina will never be like her; she's promised herself. But as they turn off the main road, down a series of twisting sandy tracks (turning with no plain design, again and again, through stickweeds and copses of damp black trees, the ocean always near, as if they were following a vein into some obscure part of the human body), she catches herself stealing glances at the rear-view mirror and thinking sentimentally of how much she loves Bobby. She might turn a corner and he would be gone, without her ever having said good-bye. Sentimental, like a black-and-white movie on late-night TV.

At the end of the end of the road is a house trailer lying on its side in the mud.

THE SUDDEN SILENCE WHEN THE ENGINES ARE SHUT OFF

"This is it," Lyle says. Tina looks around; there's no place else. She kills the engine. As Lyle gets out he turns to Bobby and yells, "Leave your lights on."

No business with the glove compartment, though, Tina notices; at least he doesn't have the gun. In the headlights of the Volvo she watches him clamber up a wooden staircase alongside the greasy bottom of the trailer, then drag himself on top—what was once the front. He opens the screen door up and the front door down and lowers himself into the hole. In a moment the porch light burns to life up on top; lights shine out the sideways windows and Lyle's head reappears through the door, like a tank captain peering out his turret. He yells, "You coming or not?"

Standing next to Bobby in the damp sand and rank salt-grass, Tina whispers, "I don't want to, Bobby. This is weird."

"We don't have to," Bobby says; then, after a minute, "I could use the money, though. He's just drunk."

"He tried to feel me up in the car."

"We'll just go," Bobby says. "We'll just get the money and go."

Neither of them moves for a few seconds. Clouds have moved in and covered the moon, a low, soft ceiling. Tina gets the feeling that the world ends at the farthest reach of the yellow porch light, an eternity of soft black nothing beyond. But then she hears, as her ears adjust to the quiet, the muffled rhythm of the surf, not far away. The yellow robs the colors, converts them to shades of gray, and again she gets the black-and-white movie feeling, the last look at a place where something happened. The wind blows through the autumn-dead leaves with a sharp, malignant rustle.

"We'll just get the money and go," Bobby says.

SIDEWAYS

Inside, the built-in furniture is all sideways, sideways sofas, sideways sinks, carpet on one wall and acoustic tile on the other, where a chandelier sags flat. A stove dangles from the ceiling. Lyle motions them to sit, a couch at right angles to the floor, so they sit on the back and rest against the seat. One of the legs of the stepladder that leads to the overhead door is resting on a poster of two nude girls in the surf at sunset, a splashing horse galloping through the shallows behind them.

Lyle reaches into the refrigerator, lying on its back on the floor, and pulls out a six-pack of midget cans.

"Instant martini," he says loudly. "Martini-in-a-can. Can I interest you?"

Before they can reply he starts throwing cans at them. One of them nearly hits Tina in the head but Bobby catches it. "Shit," Bobby says softly.

"We've got to go," Tina announces, to the room in general. She's losing track of things; she's not even scared anymore, which she knows is not right. She can't quite put anything in context. The ceiling in front of her, for instance, appears completely different now that it is presented as a wall.

Lyle wades through dishes and towels and piles of up-turned sex magazines toward them, spilling cigarette ashes as he goes. "It isn't that I don't give a shit," he says, "although I don't."

"We need to get going," Bobby says. "Why don't we settle this thing?"

(Tina witnesses the pale blobs of magazine skin crumpling under Lyle's feet, little imaginary girls.)

"You didn't even read about that storm, I bet," Lyle says. "Turned this fucker right over."

"I've got to get to work tomorrow," Bobby says. "I've got to check in by nine."

"No, you don't," Lyle says, suddenly sharp. "You don't have to be anywhere in the morning, or you wouldn't be here in the first place. Nobody's expecting you." He pops the top of the tiny can and drinks the martini off on one pull, sighs, then grins at them. "Miracles of modern technology. But I'll go get what you came for, if y'all are in that much of a hurry."

Lyle shuffles off through the wreckage, using a step stool to boost himself onto the wall of the back hallway, crawling along, dropping into one of the bedrooms with a heavy, booming sound. What would happen if he landed on a window?

"This place is creeping me out," Tina whispers.

"What's he going to do? Shoot us?" Bobby asks, annoyed. "This is like regular life. It isn't TV, it isn't the movies."

TV

The perpetrator emerged from the back of the mobile home with what we now believe is the weapon in the case (a generation of cop shows and local news taught her this language, the captain sweating in the hallway under the temporary lights, the revolver dangling from his finger). *As best we can reconstruct the incident . . .*

LYLE'S EYES

He tumbles down from the hallway wall, down into the kitchen, and when he straightens up again, she sees that he is holding the little chrome gun in his hand and that his fly is open and that his big soft cock is out.

"Watch this," he says.

He holds the pistol (both hands, the way they do on TV) and fires two bullets the length of the trailer, two messy holes in the far wall. "Nobody can hear us out here," he says, "not this time of year. Just so you know that."

There's so much to think about, the extraordinary size of his cock, like something from a different species, and the gun—where did he get it? is it the same one? did Lyle get out somehow?—yet there's so little time. Suddenly purposeful, Lyle strides quickly to Tina, wraps his free hand in her hair and forces her to her knees in front of him, while keeping the gun on Bobby. "All right, girlfriend," Lyle says. "You can do me now."

A sudden, sickening conviction sweeps through her, the knowledge that this was all her fault, that if she had been smarter or stronger or somehow better, this would never have happened, and tears of futility and rage—rage at herself, at her circumstances—began to form in her eyes.

"You think I'm fucking kidding?" Lyle says, tapping her temple with the barrel of the gun. "Take it now, girlfriend."

"Leave her alone," Bobby says quietly.

"You want it first?" Lyle says, turning toward Bobby; and in his face Tina sees an accumulation of anger, a lifetime's worth, a million dollar's worth of rage. "I'll fucking give it to you first. We've got all fucking night here."

He tosses Tina's head aside, as if he were throwing her away, sits heavily on the sofa next to Bobby and caresses his smooth head, one hand behind Bobby's neck, the other holding the pistol to his throat. As Tina's mind starts to clear (an incessant buzzing confusion of fear and anger and inability to make sense, still), she sees that Lyle's eyes are blank, and she understands, for the first time, what people mean by blind rage: he isn't seeing them at all, but a life's worth of insults and injuries. This has nothing to do with Tina and Bobby.

"Just let us go, please," she says quietly. "We won't say anything."

This enrages Lyle still further. "You think I'm fucking kidding?" he says. He raises the pistol from Bobby's neck and fires another shot through the wall behind their head, the floor, really. Tina's ears ring with the noise. "Now come on," Lyle says, pressing the barrel to Bobby's neck again, pulling his head closer.

This is like a dream, she thinks, everything so clear and sharp, and terrible things are happening, and she can't seem to move her arms or do anything about it, she can only watch: Bobby opens his mouth comically wide and takes Lyle's cock inside him, the little gun glittering like an ornament at his throat. This conjunction of flesh seems impossible, categorically wrong, and yet there it is, the physical fact, and Tina feels the dazed blankness that comes from trying to hold too many ideas at a time. A flush of anger, at Lyle specifically—at all the things he's showing her that she never wanted to see. Now Bobby seems nothing more than an extension of Lyle's cock, a toy of Lyle's desires; tears are standing on his cheeks as he starts to pump his head back and forth, slowly, and Lyle's head eases back on the worn brown sofa cushions.

Tina takes the gun from his hand, it's no more complicated than that, and puts the barrel into Lyle's mouth through his parted, pleasuring lips.

Her hands feel stiff and clumsy still in their tight-laced braces, and she can't quite understand how she got the gun from him, or what she's going to do next; only the anger, her own anger this time. She's inside Lyle now. "I ought to fucking kill you," she says.

He looks at her around the hand that's holding the gun in

his mouth, and his eyes are resigned, hidden from her. Go ahead, if you can.

Then Lyle reaches for the gun, clumsy in her stiff hands, and for a moment she thinks that he's got it again and she tries to hold on tighter to keep it from him and somehow she gets the trigger instead and squeezes and Lyle's head explodes against the wall behind him.

TINA CLOSES HER EYES

When she opens them again, none of this will have happened: she'll be lying in her bed, driving home next to Bobby, watching television.

She can still feel the cool steel of the pistol in her hand.

Suddenly she remembers the spray of blood and brains across the textured carpet behind his head, and she wheels and vomits onto the floor, dropping the gun, and vomits again, as if she could empty herself out, become blank again. As if she could remove from herself this thing she'd done.

TO THE RESCUE

"Come on, baby," Bobby says. "We'll get you out of here." One arm around her shoulders, he leads her blind to the kitchen, magazines rustling under their feet. Tina notices how quiet it has become in the trailer, and how cool. There must be a window open somewhere.

Bobby sets her down, leaning against the side of the refrigerator. When she opens her eyes she can see nothing of the main part of the living room. Bobby is staring at the blank yellow side of the refrigerator, then turns to face her, fierce. "What the fuck did you do that for?" he asks. "He's fucking dead."

Well, I hope so, Tina thinks, after all that. And then Bobby's betrayal sinks in, and she sees that he's abandoning her, and the fear kicks in, shivering in the center of her body. "I'm cold," she says.

"I don't give a shit."

She says, "I didn't . . . I didn't . . ."

She wants to say, I didn't want to, or I didn't intend to; but what she really means is I *didn't*.

"I don't care," Bobby says. "He's fucking dead. Stay here."

"Where are you going?"

"I'm going to see if I can figure something out."

"Like what?" she asks, suddenly irritated with him. But he's already gone, left her alone in the dead man's sideways kitchen. (The decedent, she remembers; the perpetrators, the incident, the decedent, the suspect.)

LYLE'S SOUL

Tina thinks it's bad luck to stay here, remembering what the Indians said: the souls of the dead are always looking for a body to ride. Stay away from the houses of the dead. She remembers this from public TV.

Although she hasn't smoked in two years, she takes an open pack of Lyle's Merits from the side of the refrigerator and lights one, taking the smoke deep into her lungs, welcoming the familiar pain and the faint dizziness that comes a moment later. I'm not sorry he's dead, she thinks—and then she's surprised when she feels that thought echo inside her, yes, yes, yes, a bone-deep satisfaction. A nameless, inappropriate anger, the anger she felt at the doctor as he laced up her arms, at Mr. Beveridge, at Bobby. Most of her is still horrified, making excuses, pretending this never happened, but somewhere inside, a voice among others, she hears herself: *Motherfucker, I'm glad you're dead.*

Then she realizes this is Lyle's soul, taking her over: helplessness turning to anger, anger turning to rage, rage turning to violence, violence turning against anyone who's handy. Not that Lyle was a bad target, exactly. But she feels herself turning into a thing she hasn't been before. "Bobby," she calls out, still sitting behind the refrigerator. "Bobby, can we get out of here now?"

No answer.

She stands up and finds herself alone, neither Lyle nor Bobby, only the spray of blood across the wall behind the sofa, or the floor. The window at the far end is open, blowing cold salt air, and she's alone, at the end of this road, waiting for the police. "Bobby," she says; then screams it: "Bobby! Bobby! Bobby!"

After a long, dull moment of panic his head pops into the window, sideways, upside-down relative to the floor, so that Tina just gives up. She doesn't know where she is.

"Let's go," Bobby says. "Bring the gun."

"Go where?" she asks, but he's gone again. She takes the crumpled pack of cigarettes, and some matches, and finally the gun (carrying it gingerly between two fingers, as if it might come to life again if she held it the right way), and follows him out the window, out into the relief of solid ground, of trees that grow from the bottom up and cars that sit on their own four wheels. Bobby's leaning against the trunk of the blue Monte Carlo, staring off into the low, soft sky. He won't look at her.

"Why?" she asks.

"Why what? You want to go to jail?"

"What are you going to do with him?"

"What are *we* going to do with him, you mean." Bobby glares, but he still isn't seeing her. It's all for effect, to keep her away. "We'll take him to the ocean," he says. "Maybe they'll never find him."

Tina tries to make herself think. "What if they catch us?" she asks.

"We've got to do something. You think of something."

"Maybe we should just call the cops," Tina says. "We didn't do anything. I mean, it was just an accident."

"You think they're going to believe us?"

"I don't know. I just want this to be over."

"You think it's worth that chance? What if they don't believe us? What happens then?"

"What happens now?" Tina asks, feeling soft and white and weak. The corridors of her body seem to echo with empty space, the night around her seems no more substantial. Nothing matters but Bobby's anger.

THE SEA

Restless in its banks, the Atlantic surges against the shore. The horizon is lit by the first faint difference of morning, far away on the metallic surface of the water.

The Monte Carlo sits a hundred yards from the edge of the water, buried up to its axles in sand. "You stupid—fucking—bitch," Tina says, resting her forehead against the cool plastic of the steering wheel, eyes closed.

"No, it's OK," Bobby says.

"I'm just so fucking stupid," she says, and he doesn't disagree. Lyle's in the trunk, morning is coming.

Bobby's Volvo waits in the safety of the turnaround at the end of the road. She can almost see it.

"We'll just have to carry him, then," Bobby says. "Give me a hand. Hurry, before it gets too light."

THE BODY OF AN ASSHOLE

Curled like damp laundry into the irregular spaces of the trunk, Lyle doesn't want to come out. Tina's nerves are sanded raw, and every approaching minute of daylight makes them worse, but nothing seems to work: he's too heavy, too cumbersome, too floppy. He has a loose-limbed grace in death that he never had in life.

Finally they pry him over the lip of the trunk, and he falls in slow motion onto the sand, one joint at a time. They each take a leg, and drag him toward the surf. Lyle's heavy. He leaves a smooth furrow of sand behind, a trail from the Monte Carlo. Every few yards they have to stop and rest; the sand is so soft and heavy that Tina feels like she may just bog down completely, collapse weeping in the sand and just wait for the cops. Not that Bobby would let her.

They reach the water and they keep walking, out into the skirts of white foam. Lyle seems to float, or maybe it's only that the water eases his slide—either way, he gets easier to pull, and they drag him out until they're both waist-deep and then let him go. The next wave carries him back to shore. Tina begins to cry.

"Shut the fuck up!" Bobby shouts over the wind and the roar of the waves. "Give me a hand."

"I just want to go home," she says. The machine is starting to break down, nerves, no sleep, no food, the poisons of last night's vodka coursing through her blood. And Lyle, looking strangely whole and clean and rested, on his side in the sand. The water is bone-deep cold, cold as a headache. The air feels warm by comparison.

They drag him deeper into the water, out beyond the breaking waves, and for a moment it seems like he'll go: he floats nine-tenths submerged, only the tips of his shoes and the moon of his belly and the soft outlines of his face above the water. Slowly, like a movie of a shipwreck, he rolls onto his side, and then face-down, drifting parallel to the shore. But then the ninth wave, the big one, catches him and sends his bones tumbling toward the sand again. Tina and Bobby watch from the shallows, weeping. Bobby's weeping too, she can see it.

Again, and again, and a fifth time they try it, each time deeper, until Tina's losing her own footing, until they are both bone-chilled with the cold Atlantic water. Bobby shoves the soft body out as far as he can; it seems to catch an undertow, and as they retreat to the shallows they can see it drifting, a little farther out with every wave. *Good-bye, Lyle,* Tina thinks. *You deserved it.* She takes the little chrome pistol from her overcoat pocket and sails it out as far as she can, where it lands with a small splash. They watch the body out of sight, shivering, then trudge the long yards back across the sand toward the Volvo past the Monte Carlo, not touching, not talking, not seeing each other.

A solitary gull stands on the edge of the open trunk of Lyle's car, pecking diligently at a dark bloodstain. Tina reaches in through the window to get the pack of cigarettes, and the gull flies off.

THE SWIMMERS

A solitary gray shark, working the shallows at daybreak, tastes blood in the water and approaches the passive floating body. Slowly, cautiously, it circles closer and closer, watching for a sign of life. No hurry for him, not this fish.

At long last he takes a fast, plunging dive at the thing, hooks the pant-leg in his razoring teeth and then lets go as Lyle's shoe jerks up and clips him under the jaw.

The shark retreats. But he doesn't surrender: he watches closely, carefully, waiting for another angle of attack, another chance—until Lyle drifts into a backwash, catches the wave that sends him tumbling to the beach again.

PEACE AND LOVE

The sun is rising behind the Texaco stations and Wal-Marts and Burger Kings, casting long, lovely shadows and yellow frames of light among the gas pumps and stop signs. They have the strip to themselves, for now. The Volvo is the same this morning as it was when the sun went down last evening: stolid, reliable. The heater is blowing hard, and Tina's hands and face are warming, but the warmth seems to stop at her skin. Nothing can penetrate her insides, where the cold seawater still chills her.

Tina starts to close her eyes, but stops herself—she knows what she'll see. She looks at her hands in their braces, filthy now with the night's work. The hands of a murderer? Maybe, Tina thinks. It doesn't seem to matter. In this lovely dawn she's reached a moment of peace.

Everything seems equal to everything else. They've made a mess of things—she can picture fingerprints everywhere, blood in the trunk of the beached Monte Carlo—but that will work itself out. She sees that events have their own current, and that she and Bobby have no choice but to be drawn along in them. But for now, for this quiet moment beyond tears, she can stand outside that endless stream of events and consequences. She can see with perfect clarity the uselessness of justice, and the need for pity: she looks at Bobby, for instance, and sees him with Lyle's cock in his mouth and a gun at his throat, and knows that she will never see him any other way, that if she ever kisses him again they will both remember, and this seems sad.

"Bobby," she says, "I love you."

He doesn't say a word. He keeps his hands on the wheel and his eyes on the road. An empty paper bag, a grocery sack, blows out into the road from one of the abandoned parking lots and Bobby swerves to avoid it but he can't—the bag is crushed under the wheels, with a loud surprising sound, then left behind them in the road. That's it, Tina thinks. That's it exactly.

junk

I WAS OUT ALL MORNING JUNKING WITH MARGARET AND HER KIDS, combing the yard sales and estate sales and rummage sales and garage sales, even some of the cheap secondhand stores. Margaret did this every Saturday. She had a business, somewhere between a business and a hobby, where she'd buy up broken small appliances, mixers, blenders, toasters, and fix them up to sell at the swap meet. It didn't seem like much but it was good for the rent on her trailer space and some pocket money besides.

This was the first time I'd spent the night with her, the first time I met her kids. It had taken us a couple of months to work our way up to it, since we met at the Vo-Tech. Margaret was in copier repair, I was in bookkeeping, which still seemed ridiculous whenever I thought about it. Shane and Alicia were dark pretty kids, Indian-looking, which they got from Margaret, who was mostly Crow Indian from up around Hardin, Montana. Shane was five and Alicia was eight and they were shy as deer mice. They shook my hand one after the other and then locked their eyes back on the cornflakes. I got the feeling this didn't happen too often, Mom bringing a man home, which was fine with me but scary.

We were both a little gun-shy, both of us still married, though I wasn't sure where my wife was that morning. I hadn't seen her in months or maybe years.

Margaret gave me a cup of instant and made me drive while she navigated a route to the sales. It was a good fall morning, with the sun just balancing over the plains, already winter in the shadows, the cottonwood trees losing their leaves and the aspens turning yellow. A morning breeze was blowing the refinery haze out of the valley and the sky was almost blue. We were early birds, garage-sale pirates, and I felt fine. I woke up with a dream of myself where I would get my job back at the carbon black plant or maybe go out strip-mining up north and then set up housekeeping. I liked the company of women and children, I'd almost forgotten how much.

Margaret had a deadly eye. Some places she wouldn't even let me stop, others she'd dart for the pile of junk they hadn't sorted out yet, rooting through the puzzles and picture frames and orphan silverware. She'd go a dollar for a blender, fifty cents for a toaster. The sellers would take it, almost always, no matter how optimistic the price was on the masking-tape tag—they knew she was a professional. Fifteen dollars for a broken mixer, seven-fifty for a popcorn machine that only blew cold air, these prices were the dreams of greed when Margaret came to the yard sale. "Junk," she'd say, holding a blender by the cord and scowling at it. "I'll go a buck."

Part of my mind was on the side of the sellers. I knew what they were thinking: look how much of this thing is perfectly fine, look at how much still works perfect—the mixer bowls, both the original beaters, all this chrome and enameled steel—it *should* be worth more. Only a little part of this is broken. It isn't right, I could hear them thinking. I'm being took. They got it confused, to where it was more about pride than money.

"I don't think so," this one woman told her. "For that kind of money, I guess I'd just as soon keep it." Clutching her little busted mixer, like Margaret had tried to steal it from her.

Margaret just shrugged her shoulders and got in the car. There was another broken mixer someplace. Maybe some optimist would come along and pay the asking price, I thought, though it didn't seem likely. Sell it or get stuck with it.

By two o'clock the garage sales had dried up and Margaret had filled the trunk of her Subaru with broken toasters. It was a big day for toasters. Time to take the kids to McDonald's. They were worn out from the effort of being good all morning and they didn't have anything to show for it, so it was the Happy

Meal. They sat in the corner booth and the whole town was passing by them, Saturday afternoon at McDonald's, everybody knew everybody else and they were talking. I lifted one corner of the bun and looked down at the gray circle of meat. "Do you suppose it's true?" I asked.

"What?" Alicia said.

"The thing they say about the meat, where it comes from?"

"Don't be smart-ass around my kids," Margaret said. I thought she was kidding at first, but I looked up and she was looking at me cold serious through the heavy black glasses she wore and I thought she looked beautiful, defending her children, like some wild thing. "They get enough of that at school," she said, "all the smart-ass about everything. What's in here is just regular cow meat."

"From Brazil," I said.

"Kids have to believe in something," Margaret said. "They can't just believe in nothing."

Shane paid no attention to his mom and asked me, "What did they say was in the hamburger?"

"You never mind," Margaret said, and gave me a look. I wanted to ask her, Just because you have to believe in something, does that mean you have to believe in McDonald's? But I didn't. It was good to see her standing up for her kids even if she was wrong. She looked beautiful when she was angry like that. Sitting in Mickey D's in the smell of french-fry grease, I thought about how beautiful she was: long dark hair and a long neck, thin, with that Crow wildness in her face. She was good-looking to where her looks could get her in trouble, which is what happened when she was nineteen and afterward for a while. So I heard.

"It was rat, wasn't it?" Shane asked. "They put rat in the hamburgers."

"You shut up and eat," Margaret said. "Parker didn't mean anything like that."

"That's right," I said, although that was exactly what I was going to say. Not that I actually thought there was rat in the hamburgers, but it would impress the kids. Plus you couldn't tell what was in there by looking.

Alicia lifted the corner of her bun and looked in and then looked at her brother. "You are a disgusting human being," she said. "I wash my hands of you."

"All right, enough," Margaret said. "Sit up and eat, sit up!" And when the kids were eating their hamburgers again, she turned to me, serious again. "No more kids," she said quietly, for adults to hear. "I've got two kids and my husband was a kid and it just wears me out, OK? Do you know what I mean?"

"Yeah I do."

"I don't mind a little smart-ass, not from you," she said, blinking at me through her glasses. "I mean, you've got to be good for something."

"Well thanks, I guess."

"I don't know if it was a compliment or not," she said. "Eat your hamburger." And she wasn't looking at me then and I don't know what she meant or how she meant it, but I felt this warmth all around my body, like I was inside of something, some kind of bubble or cloud with me and Margaret and the kids inside it, and I liked that feeling. Like it wasn't me that was sitting there but some other man who was lucky about these things, lucky about love and about people.

And then we were gone out of there and Margaret was dropping me off at my room at the Sacajawea Apartments and

I saw the turquoise Thunderbird from down the block. It was Dorothy's car, my wife. She had that car since high school, a '66, with a white interior and a white vinyl top, a beautiful thing. I noticed that she had Arizona plates on it now, with the little cactus in the middle. I could see the back of her blond head.

"You want to come out to the swap meet tomorrow?" Margaret asked. "I'll pick you up if you want."

"I'll call you," I said. Suddenly I was nervous to get rid of her, not for her, just so I could think clearly. I was trying to remember how long it had been since I saw Dorothy. Over a year anyway. Two years? Suddenly I was bookkeeping again.

Margaret said, "Well, I can't get hold of you, so call me if you want to go."

She leaned across the front seat and kissed me, right in front of the kids, and we both said good-bye, good-bye, while I got out of the car. I couldn't even think about them. I watched her little Subaru roll down the street and around the corner, but really I was waiting for the door of the Thunderbird to open. Which it did.

One of the things about Dorothy was that whoever made up these Western girl clothes had her in mind exactly. She had on a fringe jacket and spray-on jeans tucked into her boots and she was smoking a cigarette. She was older, though, which was a surprise. There were dark circles under her eyes and wrinkles around her mouth, and you could really tell it by her hands. I saw this with a kind of panic—this was never sup-posed to happen—as she walked up to me slowly with a grin on her face, not too nice.

"Who's the squaw?" she said.

This was her style, ice water in the face. I stood there

blinking for a minute, wondering whether to slap her, and then I remembered: if I slapped her, I lost. Life with Dorothy was one long game of cool.

She said, "I never pictured you as a family man, exactly."

"I just met the woman," I said, although I'd known Margaret for three months then.

"That isn't what it looked like," Dorothy said. "It looked like Mom and Dad on the way to work. Can I come in?"

She didn't wait for an answer but went into the hallway and waited for me to show her which door was mine. And then it was like she never left.

"Jesus, Parker," she said, looking around the little room: one bed, one chair, a TV, a desk with my books from the Vo-Tech on it. "Are you sure this is depressing enough? Is that a bloodstain?"

She pointed to a blotch on the wall that I'd wondered about myself. But I said, "No, it's just rust or something."

"Well, it looks like blood to me. Have you got a beer?"

She didn't wait but opened up the little dormitory refrigerator and took the last beer and opened it. She drank it like a drowning man, half at once. Then sat down at the table and started chopping out a line of something, crank I guessed, onto my one clean dinner plate. A little silver hunting knife with lumps of turquoise in the handle was the weapon. She chopped it fine and then took a hit in each side of her nose off the sharp point of the blade. Tears welled up in her eyes as she shook her head. "Jesus, that's good," she said. "A little eye-opener. Want some?"

"No, thanks."

"Suit yourself," she said, dipping the point of the blade into the crank again and lining it up her nose. I watched her

73

like a hungry dog watching a person eat, following the point of the knife with my eyes. I'm not that kind of person anymore, I told myself. I'm done with that.

Eyes still shut, making a face from the pain of the hit, she said, "I need some money, Parker. I'm sort of in trouble."

Fuck you, I thought, and then I said it: "Fuck you." Back in town for thirty seconds and already we were playing by her rules and my own life had shrunk to nothing. "You come around here," I said, trying to find the words. "I haven't even seen you for a year and a half . . ."

She just looked at me calm and straight-faced until the words dried up completely. "I wouldn't ask you if I didn't need your help," she said. "You know that."

"So what?"

"I'm just asking for mine," she said.

"What do you mean?" I asked her. "Are you talking about the house?" She looked up, and it was the house, and I started to laugh.

"I'm not kidding you," Dorothy said. "I was your wife for all the time we were making payments on that place. I'm entitled to something."

"You never put a nickel into that house," I said, still laughing. "I mean, don't bullshit me. But it don't matter anyway."

"What do you mean?"

"That money's gone, darling. That money was gone a year ago."

She was all business now, a skinny mean-faced woman, just the way I always liked her. She asked me, "Where exactly did the money go?"

"I don't know, darling," I said, and there was a kind of

74

glory in it. This was not a regular mistake but a big one, a disaster, and I felt a kind of roller-coaster excitement at the memory. Nothing that was good for you. I said, "Most of it I can't remember."

"That was thirty-two thousand dollars," Dorothy said.

"Not after the lawyers got their cut—the lawyers, and then the neighborhood association that started the lawsuit got a percentage. And then a big chunk of the rest went into that idiot Ford pickup. You know I wrecked it."

She shook her head.

"Put it around somebody's mailbox out by Ripton. I didn't total it but pretty close."

"You didn't have insurance on it?"

"They canceled me out a couple of days before. I guess I didn't pay the bill. I don't know. I never found the letter. But then when the bank took the pickup back, I had to pay the difference. That and the Visa bill we ran up, and after that I don't know. I mean, it went somewhere, I guess. It's gone."

"Thirty-two thousand dollars," she said again, and thought about it for a minute. "Jesus, Parker, you spent that money like it was a dime."

I bobbed my head, like she had just paid me a compliment, and it felt like that: this was the one thing I'd done, the thing they couldn't take away from me. This was the only time I'd ever be bigger than life.

"That was it," I said. "The house, the truck, I quit showing up for work over at the carbon black plant and they canned my ass over there. Did you hear about the guy who played the country record backwards?"

Dorothy shook her head.

"He got his job back, he got his dog back, he got his wife back . . ." I looked down and noticed that Dorothy's hands were trembling. She was holding one of her hands just off the tabletop and watching it shake, like it was somebody else's hand. "What's the matter, baby?" I asked.

"I'm not your baby."

"Whatever you are."

"I'm not kidding about being in trouble," she said. "Your buddy Coy, up here, he's in with a rough crowd."

"How long have you been in town?"

"I've been in and out, the last few months."

I sat on the edge of the bed wondering how I missed her in a town this small, while she went on looking at her hands. I was thinking about Coy, my high school buddy, old junkie friend. I hadn't seen Coy in a while, imagined him fucking Dorothy. I asked her, "What does Coy have to do with it?"

"Oh, fuck you," she said. "I didn't come here to explain myself, I came because I was in trouble and I was hoping you could help me out. I guess I was wrong."

She started to fold the powder back into the little paper envelope and I didn't want her to go. I don't know why, I just have to try to put it together, looking back. I could have let her go and none of the rest of it would have happened, and my reasons, when I try to put them together, are not all that good. Part of it was that I expected to fuck her, not exactly that I wanted to, although I did. But every time since high school there was always that charge, the one constant. Our bodies fit each other and I knew that if I touched her, if she let me inside, we would be the same as we ever were. If she left, the chain was broken, that part of my life was over and I'd be left behind with the others—the good students, churchgoers, bookkeepers. I didn't want to be ditched, maybe it was simple as that.

Nobody to blame but myself.

"What do you need?" I asked her.

That next day, Margaret took me along with the kids out to the big swap meet at the Go West drive-in, four hundred cars packed in backwards on the humps, card tables and milk crates, an old turkey-necked buzzard with one cardboard box only, a hole cut in the top: XXX VIDEOS U-PICK $5.00. I was tired and spaced and it was a lie for me to be there. Setting up the folding tables, setting out the popcorn makers and blenders that Margaret brought to sell, I remembered the tangle of Dorothy's legs and mine and the taste of her neck and the burn of the crank as it went down, the old pain and then the rush. But it was a cool clear day with a breeze and after a while my blood started to move. Actually I started to like it.

My job was to hold down the fort, along with Alicia, while Shane and Margaret scoured the back rows for fixable junk. There wasn't any clear line between buyers and sellers at the Go West. Half the business was trades, my junk for your junk, but there was quite a bit of movement here, quite a bit of life. This was hope of a practical kind, people trying to get somewhere. I was a spy in their house, a double agent. I was sitting in my chair watching them and keeping my secrets: Dorothy's laughter and her voice, *Bookkeeping? Bookkeeping?* Jesus, Parker, that's funny . . . There is no other life, I wanted to tell them, the person that you are is the person you're going to be. Though it was tempting to pretend. Something beautiful in all the movement, all the scurrying around in the clear light, buying and selling, moving forward.

But it was stupid, too, and it wasn't hard to make fun of them: the rusty mag wheels and broken bicycles and cassette tapes in Mexican, the sharp eyes of the bargainers. "This thing work?" they ask, holding up a ten-dollar blender, shaking it, listening for rattles.

"Works fine."

"Mind if I plug it in?"

"I'll get it for you." Then Sherlock Holmes investigates, listening for rattles, trying all twelve speeds: LIQUEFY, PUREE, FRAPPÉ.

"I guess I could go seven and a half," Sherlock says.

"This isn't my booth," I tell him, as instructed. "I can't go lower than nine on my own, but if you want to come back later . . ." He shakes his head, doubtfully. "You could give it a try."

"You guarantee it?"

"If it doesn't work, bring it back next week, we'll give you another." Sherlock still can't make up his mind, so I try to encourage him: "Margaret's here every week."

"This's Margaret's booth?" Sherlock looks around at the stuff and grins. "Course it is, who else would it be—stupid of me, getting stupid. Well, you tell Margaret that Frank Teller's got her blender, and if she wants to make a deal with me she can come see me." Sherlock leaves with the blender under his arm, which seems to be OK with Alicia—she shrugs at me, elaborately.

When Margaret got back with a load of broken toasters, it was OK with her, too, though she immediately went out to track down the deal. She looked happy and purposeful in the hard sunlight. The drive-in was scurrying with things and shoppers, like an ant farm busying itself against the last days before winter, which this might have been. The night before with Dorothy felt like a dream in the hard clear light. It made me happy to be a part of the life, minding the store in my folding lawn chair, making change out of a cigar box, watching the 49ers on a little five-inch black-and-white with Alicia, who was rooting for the Broncos.

"John Elway," she said, serious as ever. "The three amigos. They can't lose."

"It doesn't really matter who wins," I told her, I guess because it sounded like the kind of thing an adult ought to say. "The important thing is the game, not the winner."

Alicia looked at me like I was nuts. *"Somebody's* got to win," she said. "And somebody's got to *lose."*

"Yeah, well," I said, answerless, and tried to interest myself in the game.

Margaret cleared $153 that afternoon, not counting what she had to spend for broken junk. She took us out for hamburgers at Stockman's Cafe downtown, then the three of them dropped me off at my room and we all made a lot of plans and promises I couldn't even remember later on.

I couldn't remember because Coy was waiting for me along with Dorothy when I got back to my room and somebody had beaten the shit out of Coy. She was washing his face, which was a mess, bruises rising up around his eyes, lips like burned Vienna sausages, and I looked over at my schoolbooks on the little desk and wondered what the fuck I was doing in the middle of this. *Books for Business* and the *Cash Flow Work Book.*

"What happened to him?" I asked Dorothy.

"His friends happened to him," she said. "The same ones that are going to happen to me if I don't come up with twenty-five hundred dollars."

"Maybe the two of you should leave town," I said. But when I said it I saw Coy and Dorothy fucking again, I saw how tenderly she held the washcloth to Coy's damaged face, and I couldn't stand to let her go. I'm doing this for love, I thought. It seemed like enough of a reason.

"I'm going to Denver," Coy said, though it was hard to understand him because of how swollen up his face was. "I fuck to share."

"What?" I asked him.

"I'm fuckin' *scared* of those guys," Coy said. He leaned his head back in the chair until he was looking at Dorothy upside down, behind him. He said, "I'm fuckin' scared of you, too. Shit like this didn't used to happen to me," or maybe he said "doesn't usually happen to me." I couldn't tell. There was a minute of quiet between them in the kitchen where I could feel it slipping away: the swap meet, Margaret, the busy bees getting ready for winter.

The kitchen light was too bright, too clear. I didn't want to see that clearly. When I switched it off, a soft, late-afternoon light came through the dirty window that put us all in twilight. Even Coy's hamburger face looked like it was out of an old painting, the way he looked back at Dorothy, the way she looked down at him. I felt like the light was connecting all of us, holding us in a fold like a soft gray cloth. The place where the world balances, I thought, not knowing exactly what I meant. And a line from an old song: *she loves me better than I love myself.*

"I'm going to Denver," Coy said, and got up out of the chair and got his jacket from the couch and got out the little chrome automatic that was between the sofa cushions. It had been a while since I'd seen a gun and it came as a surprise. "I'm gone," he said, holding the pistol toward Dorothy, grip first. "You want this?"

"Maybe I'd better," she said, and tucked it into her white purse with the long leather fringes, and took her lipstick out while she was in there and freshened up in a little mirror she carried.

And then Coy was gone and it was old times again: she laid the little pistol on the counter and a pint of vodka and a pack of Virginia Slims and the mirror and the knife and the little paper envelope. Like a kit, I thought, a Dorothy kit. "Did I tell you about the radioactive mud?" she asked me.

"I don't remember," I said.

"You'd remember if I told you," she said. "At least I hope you would. It was this resort place down near Phoenix, kind of a shithole, you know, run-down, but it must have been nice once. And anyway, they were dumb enough to give me a job . . ."

I eased back in the kitchen chair and it was just like three in the morning, even though it wasn't even five in the afternoon yet. I reached a beer out of the little dorm refrigerator while she told her story. This is what love means, I thought: the thing you can't walk away from. It was just like old times.

And then it was three in the morning for real and I was by myself again in the one-room apartment and I couldn't sleep.

Partly it was the crank but mostly it was the old tightrope-walker feeling I got from Dorothy, looking down and seeing the ground so far below . . . Before she left I gave her a check for the $2,500, a good check, but it was most of the money I had in the world. She gave me the keys to the turquoise Thunderbird but I knew I couldn't sell it. It was just a loan, a temporary thing, there was no need to transfer the title.

Thinking about this, it was like I had two parts of my brain and one side was always trying to bullshit the other and always succeeding. It was like the old days when every morning I would wake up and say that was the day I was going to quit and every day I was back on the crank by noon. The best part would be when I'd promise myself I was going to quit the next day, and then I'd just do up everything in the house, all the crank, drink all the whiskey, smoke all the cigarettes, so I wouldn't be tempted . . . The funny part was that one side of my brain really did know what was going on. One side of my brain knew that I'd pissed away the money for rent and food and tuition at the Vo-Tech and it was really gone.

It was all for today. Dorothy was not going to get beat up. It felt crazy, the way that months of my future went down the toilet to pay for good times she already had, good times she had without me. I thought of how I made that money one day at a time: working on the railroad, an extra gang out of St. Regis, Montana. I was swinging a nine-pound spike maul ten hours a day and liking it. After a few weeks the foreman offered to let me switch to machine operator but I told him no, thanks. I liked the feel of the hammer, liked the feeling of getting strong and sleeping well.

The one side of my brain knew what the truth was and

the other side had just lies and bullshit: Dorothy would come through, it didn't matter anyway, something would have happened to throw me back into the old life if it wasn't her . . . What made me feel crazy was that I was acting like the truth was nothing and the lies and the bullshit were real. The truth was cold and hard and it was easier to look the other way or to pretend, but that didn't keep it from being the truth. That railroad money was going to pay for a new life and now it was gone. I was miles above the ground, looking down, crazy. I thought of the work that I had put into that money. I thought of how long it would take Margaret to make that money with her toasters and blenders and it made me sick, sick in my body. I pulled on my wool coat and my stupid hat with the flaps. I had to get out of this room.

An ice fog and a refinery haze blanketed the street outside and made the air taste like gasoline. The Thunderbird stood at the curb, the windshield blind with ice. The dings and dents stood out in the yellow light, and you could see the old uneven Bondo job in the back wheel wells. I asked for water, I thought, and she gave me gasoline. Sometimes the blues made perfect sense, three in the morning and drifting down the empty streets, looking for something. Dead leaves rustled in the gutters, like lawyer's papers. Drifting: my feet would take me anywhere but I couldn't tell which way to go. Every direction was as good as any other and the blues came up inside again: I'm just drifting and drifting, baby, like a ship out on the sea . . . out in the night and praying for a lighthouse, a signal from shore, anything to tell the rocks from the harbor, crazy . . . My feet took me toward the old neighborhood, where the streetlights ended. Since the company bought the houses up they had gone abandoned and dark. The high school kids shot out the windows and stole the plumbing and painted their names in spray-can splashes and drips, like they pissed red paint onto the wall. TOXIC HAZARD, read the notices on every door, DANGER PELIGRO.

I turned the corner onto my old block and it was like a mouthful of broken teeth, with the glass still hanging in the window frames and the dark holes where the doors were hammered down. There were winos living in some of these places. I could see Sterno flames flickering on the walls, on the street where I learned to ride a bicycle, fell in love, where my mother and my father celebrated their anniversaries one after the other until the gasoline got into the ground water. That was where things started turning to shit: when the gasoline started coming through the basement walls. I was still high off Dorothy's crank and I could see everything perfectly clearly, I could see my own life for once. And this street was where my life was, where I had a job and a wife and a $21,000 pickup truck with a stereo that would blow the fucking doors off. And then what? The gasoline dissolved the paint so it came off the basement walls in big rubbery sheets and then Dorothy left and since then I didn't know where I was going. Somewhere there was a connection. I was feeling sorry for myself. I tried to stop, I called myself a pussy, but there was something missing, just gone, and the emptiness and lonely feeling would not leave me be.

A flickering candlelight was coming from the window of my old living room, and a sound of voices. I edged up toward the house across the battered grass, gone to dirt now, mostly. Trying not to make any noise, I found out how drunk I was. I tripped over a clump of dirt and the voices quit inside. After a minute they started up again and I crept up closer, trying to make out the words, but they fell away in scraps on the cold wind. One of the voices belonged to a woman and suddenly I knew it was Dorothy.

I crept up closer, wondering what she was doing there, what she was cooking up, who she was fucking. It came to me like somebody turning on a light: she was going to spend my money and she was going to fuck somebody else and I was going to be out in the cold, always. I pictured her singing in the broken house, sharing a pint of whiskey, the bitch. It wasn't even love, it was just a game I couldn't quit playing, or maybe it was the same thing . . . Everything felt so clear and sharp to me but nothing made sense.

I stuck my head through the window and it wasn't Dorothy at all but a dark-haired woman, maybe an Indian. For a minute I thought of Margaret but then I saw that I didn't know anything at all.

"The fuck out of here," one of the men shouted, and I ran down my own lawn and through the dark, fear mixing with the taste of gasoline in the air. Through the dark and running, and after a minute I liked the feel of running, the punishment I was giving my body. My lungs were suffering, my legs were burning, my face was turning to glass in the cold, and it was fine with me. I knew I deserved it, I deserved worse and sooner or later I'd get it. The thoughts came in rhythm with my pumping legs: I don't need this trouble, I don't want this trouble, don't save this trouble for anyone but me . . . Running slowly now, with the crank and alcohol pumping through my blood, I felt like I was about to fall down under a streetlight and that was all right too, whatever happened. I saw myself frozen dead in the weeds and maybe that was what was supposed to happen. The streets were too wide, the people who lived here now weren't big enough to fill them up, I wasn't big enough.

I didn't stop until I got to Margaret's trailer. I leaned against a boat-tail Riviera parked across the street and I stared at the dark windows, breathing hard. I didn't know what I wanted from her but I knew that I wanted her, and when I saw the light go on in her bedroom I thought that I'd woken her up with my thoughts.

"Parker, is that you?" she asked. "What are you doing out here?"

I tried to think of what I ought to say, watching her eyes blink, trying to see. A little bit of a moon that night. She was wearing a down jacket and sno-pacs over her nightgown, and her hair was tangled and loose.

"I don't really have an explanation," I finally said.

"Did you want to see me?"

"No," I said, and I could see her face was still confused, full of sleep. "I mean, I want to see you, but I don't think you want to see me."

"That's too much to think about," she said. "It's time to sleep now. Do you want to come in with me?"

"Do you want me to?"

"I'm standing here in my nightgown," she said. "This is stupid."

She took my hand in hers and led me up the little stairs into her trailer. We took our coats off and then our boots and she led me down the narrow hall, to her bed all the way at the back. I wanted to cry and it wasn't just the whiskey: I was full of thanks, so happy to be forgiven. Margaret folded herself back under the covers, watching with her dark eyes as I fumbled with my clothes.

"Don't do this again," she whispered. "I can't do it, not with the kids."

"I won't," I promised, and I meant it. That night, I felt like Dorothy was the last mistake of the person I used to be. I was full of plans, the future inside me, bursting to get out.

"You will," she whispered. "Come here."

There were two more days after that, a Monday and a Tuesday, regular days. Margaret gave me a ride to the Vo-Tech in her little Datsun truck and then I took the bus back to her trailer while she picked the kids up from school and ran the usual errands. I stayed away from the Sacajawea—I didn't want to see Dorothy and I didn't know what the chances were, whether she was already gone or what else she might want from me. I was worn out with her.

The weather turned cold and the wind blew hard out of the north, making Margaret's trailer tremble on its base. We'd spend the winter nights around her kitchen table, drinking coffee and fixing Mr. Coffees and FryBabys and Mixmasters. She'd do the motors and switches herself, but she'd let me take things apart and put them back together, while the kids cleaned the cases, using Liquid Secretary to cover spots and stains. She'd shut the TV off when the kids went to bed, then we'd pack all the spare motors back into the milk crates, the tools into her fancy copier-repair tool briefcase, pack it all away and work on our homework for an hour or so in the quiet, not talking. Watch a little TV, maybe have a beer.

Now those winter nights stand for something, I don't know—like part of a whole life, like a little patch cut from a big bolt of cloth. There was a whole everyday life of chores and reasonable plans and comfort, but those were the only days of it we ever got to live. I feel like I can remember every minute, but there's nothing to remember: breakfast, dinner, television, work, Shane and Alicia singing "John Jacob Jingleheimer Smith" until we were both ready to murder them.

The third day was a Wednesday. Margaret had an early class but I didn't have to be there till noon. I let her go early and hung around the trailer for a while by myself, drinking coffee and reading the Nickel Ads: firewood, computers, four-wheel drives. I tried to figure out what the Thunderbird was worth but there was nothing in the paper, and besides, I didn't even have the title. After a minute I had to stop thinking about it because I felt the craziness again.

Around ten-thirty I walked over to the Sacajawea to check the mail and get some clothes, taking the long way around to stay out of the way of the old neighborhood. The Thunderbird was still parked out front when I got there, which was not quite a surprise. I changed my clothes and showered and shaved and started to feel pretty good. My schoolbooks were still there in the room but I wasn't too far behind. I decided it would be easier to study in the library of the Vo-Tech instead of my room, and then I decided to take the Thunderbird to school instead of the bus. Maybe Margaret wouldn't see me, or maybe I would explain it to her. Maybe I just didn't think about it, which is how it feels now, trying to figure out why.

The Thunderbird started right up and ran strong. I'd forgotten what it was like to drive, with the big, powerful V-8 and the power steering and power brakes and automatic—a big smooth ride, a mile of turquoise hood out in front of me and the big chrome dashboard with the Indian symbols. I punched the buttons on the radio till I found a rock song, "All Right Now," and turned it up and tapped my fingers on the steering wheel in time to the music. I felt fast, dangerous, untouchable. Even at the Vo-Tech, the high kept up. I kept looking back at the Thunderbird on my way into the building, the best-looking car in the parking lot, nothing but trouble but it was mine, for now anyway.

The two bikers came into the library about half an hour later. I knew they were looking for me, even before I saw one of the front-office staff pointing me out. They both had beards and little black braids. One of them was only big, while the other one was huge, three hundred pounds or more.

The one who was only big said, "Look, we need to get the keys from you."

"What keys?" I said.

"Let's not bullshit this," the biker said. "I mean seriously. Dorothy owes us the money, give us the keys, we'll call it quits, OK?"

And the keys were in my pocket and I could have just given them up, taken them out, handed them over, and that would have been it—no car, no money, no wife and no future life that was any different. And all of this had already happened, and part of it was that I couldn't admit it to myself. I just felt empty and stupid. It was like looking down from a high place: I felt like I could see it all, my whole life at once. And for some reason at that moment I thought of Shane and

Alicia and how I had come from being a child to being here, and the waste of that child's life, and I couldn't do it. With the car I had something, some kind of hope, even if it was a lie. Otherwise there was just nothing.

"That's not your car," I said.

"The fuck it's not," the biker said.

"I have a receipt," I said, sounding puny even to myself. I thought, Here it comes. Part of me wanted it, whatever was going to happen next.

But it was nothing. The biker clapped his hands down on the library table with a loud sound that made the other students stare, and he leaned down to look into my eyes and said, "I wish you'd quit trying to be an asshole about this."

He had a low, raspy voice but he wasn't trying to make it mean. It sounded almost like he cared. I could smell the complicated stink coming off the biker, leather and hair grease and cigarette smoke. I knew a couple of bikers around town and they were good guys to have as friends, good to drink with, but sometimes they told stories about this other life, the part that I wasn't allowed into, girls and trains and pool cues. And the other thing was just a dream, there was nothing real about the Thunderbird. But there was nothing real about any of the rest of it, nothing for me.

"Sorry," I said, and left the keys in my pocket.

"It's going to get worse," the biker said, and stood up, and both of them walked out.

I was shaking inside and the other students were staring at me. I collected my books and went to the window, where I could just see the bumper of the Thunderbird. I expected them just to steal it and I almost wished they would, just get it over with.

Ten minutes passed and the car was still there and I was still there, holding my books in my arms like a high school girl. It was a cold gray day, with a wind blowing papers across the parking lot. The snow was melted off everywhere but the shadows of the trees and I was thinking that it was time to quit —time to move on and give it another try somewhere else. Except for trips to here and there, I'd lived in this town for my whole life and I couldn't help thinking I'd made a mess of it. I tried to hate Dorothy for the mess she made but it was my fault as much as hers. I just wish that I had thought of this ten minutes earlier, so I could have given the two bikers the keys to the Thunderbird and gotten the whole thing over with.

What happened was I left my schoolbooks on one of the tables in the library and went off to find Margaret. It was noontime, so I expected to find her in the cafeteria and she was, head-down over her books, drinking cafeteria coffee along with the brown-bag lunch she brought from home. This was the way I first saw her, and really I can't remember if what I'm telling you is the memory of that particular day or just the way she was. Anyway, she was surprised to see me when I tapped her on the shoulder.

"What are you doing here, Parker?" she asked. "I thought you had a class."

"I did," I said. "I wanted to explain something."

"Like what?" She took her glasses off and rubbed her eyes and looked at me, suspicious. But she must have seen the trouble in me because she changed. "Sit down," she said.

But I couldn't tell her about Dorothy, there in the cafeteria —it was too bright, too normal, too much in the light of day. What I really needed was three in the morning, a couple of drinks, but I had the feeling that I didn't have time for that.

"Come with me for a second," I asked her, and after a minute she said yes. She gathered her books and followed me out into the cold noontime and over to the Thunderbird.

"Whose car is this?" she asked when she saw me open the door with the key. "Who does this belong to?"

"It's mine for now," I told her, and opened the lock on the other door. She hesitated for a minute before she got in, and I remember that I was angry with her—like she didn't trust me, like I was fooling her all along. "Come on," I said, and started the engine.

She got in, fumbled around for a seat belt before she realized the car was too old to have them. She looked at all the beautiful chrome, the white leatherette. "Where did this come from?" she asked.

"It's a long story," I said. I backed the car out of the space and headed for the exit, and Margaret was looking at me from across the seat, a long ways away, like she'd never seen me before.

"Where are you going?" she asked.

"I just want to get away from here for a minute," I said, easing the car out into the traffic on 34th Street, heading west, toward the mountains. I waited a few more blocks, until she was settled back into her seat instead of pressed against the door like she was trying to get away from me, and then I told her: "I'm in all kinds of trouble."

"What do you mean?" she asked.

"I think I might have to go away for a while," I said. I was going to tell her about Dorothy, and about the mess I made, but even at that last minute I didn't want to. It was like saying the words would make them real, and as long as I didn't say them the trouble would go away by itself, like a little balloon flying off.

"There's somebody waving at you," Margaret said.

I looked over two lanes and there were the bikers in a blue Chevy pickup and the one that had done the talking was in the passenger side with the window down, waving his hand for me to stop. I slowed down at first, and the traffic carried them past me and I started looking for a place to turn.

"What's going on, Parker?" Margaret asked, but I was trying to think and I didn't answer. I looked over and the blue pickup was drifting back toward me through the other cars. I thought that I could get into the parking lot of a gas station but the pickup cut me off, and then I gave the Thunderbird some gas and we shot around them and we were off to the races, Margaret cursing in the seat beside me, cursing at me, God damn you, Parker, stop this fucking car. And after that I can't really sort it out, except that we went back and forth through the traffic and I thought I could make a quick turn and then get away and then Margaret gave this new sound and I looked over and the biker was pointing a sawed-off shotgun at my head. I gunned the engine to get out of the way and went through the red light at Highland and then there was this sound, I don't know, metal and screaming and tires where the Cadillac tried to stop before he plowed into the passenger side. She lived, though the glass made a mess of her face. Her hipbone broke into pieces and still hasn't mended, that's what I hear. I don't know. I don't see her, except in my sleep. I see the last thing, Margaret hanging like a red doll out the hole in the windshield and then the steering wheel breaking apart in my hands and then, most of the time, I wake up.

moonbeams and aspirin

ON THE VERGE OF DIVORCE, THEY HEADED FOR FLORIDA: AN ISLAND in the Gulf, a place they remembered as a refuge, dolphins, pelicans, vodka–and–Cheez Whiz picnics. They'd never been there in high season before, though. The roads were overrun with ice-cream-colored Cadillacs and Lincolns, Hoosiers in golf clothes, Buckeyes and Badgers and Show-Me's.

The last room on the island was next to the dock at the marina. The returning fishermen would park themselves outside the window every noon and boom at each other, driving Lockhart and Margaret from their beds, groping for aspirin and sunglasses. They began to feel hunted. Driving from restaurant to restaurant, searching for a late breakfast, they were crowded out by throngs of grinning well-off people who had been up since seven, who hadn't known a hangover since college. Not that drinking was solving anything, exactly.

And something was killing the fish: the dredge, was Lockhart's theory, anchored a hundred yards offshore and pumping streams of sand to replace the beach, which a winter storm had washed away. Every wave of the low Gulf tide brought ashore more dead fish, which had begun to smell. Half the island was uninhabitable.

Irritated and confused, they drove around in a rented pink Jeep. The only thing Lockhart was learning was how much he would miss her. They had nothing but each other's company; it was almost enough. The third day they found a little empty notch of beach, protected by a line of island pines, where the water was clear and the black-backed dolphins swam close to shore, breaking the water with their fins. Margaret read Jackie Collins, reading the worst sentences aloud. Lockhart went snorkeling and saw a beach under the water that looked exactly like the beach above the water. They swam, they drank sweet white wine, they didn't talk. A perfect afternoon. Lockhart was sorry to see it end. Waist-deep in the tepid water of the Gulf, alone, they watched the sun set through clouds: castles of fire, golden hillsides.

"What if we stayed together?" he asked her.

"Don't confuse me," she said. "I just want to be here, in this moment, right now, OK?"

Lockhart had nothing to say; technically, this was all his fault.

They stayed in the water until the moon came up, water and air the same temperature, pelicans flying through the evening, dark shapes against the dark sky. Lockhart tried to kiss her; she splashed ashore, pulled a dress on over her wet suit. The moon lit the path back through the woods. The Jeep sat at the edge of the road, the first step on a trip he didn't want to take, back to their lives, back into history. Lockhart wanted to stand naked, just the two of them, without words if they could manage it. Instead they drove, a car among other cars, searching for a late dinner among the cheerful throngs.

Traffic thinned as they drove the narrow thread of the road, past the bright resorts and busy restaurants, toward the vast blankness of the Gulf. Long stretches of darkness intervened between the villages of neon, lanes of little snug cottages. Lockhart thought of all the happy people in their cottages, all the happy evenings, knowing he was making it up. This end of the island was dark, deserted, the headlights of the pink Jeep cutting crazy shadows in the dense roadside greenery, sword plants and elephant ears and lianas. At the edge of the last parking lot stood a large grass shack of yellow cement: the Luau Hut. "Is this all right?" he asked her.

"What?" She was miles away, slowly coming into focus, looking around. "Well," she said, "I guess this will have to do."

She held her arm out toward the emptiness of the Gulf, all around them, as if she meant this to be an argument for something.

The dining room of the Luau Hut was half-busy but the bar was empty; they chose the bar, ordering gin and Bong-Bong Chicken Wings and not talking, still damp with salt water. After a round of drinks, a blind man came in with his dog.

"You can't bring that dog in here," the bartender said. "Is that your dog? You can't bring him in here."

"You must be new here," the blind man said, hoisting himself onto a barstool kitty-corner from Lockhart and Margaret. The big German shepherd curled at his feet. "It's a seeing-eye dog. Now get me a double old-fashioned on the rocks and a glass of water. Thank you."

The bartender glared at the blind man, glared at the dog, elaborately shrugged his shoulders and set to work. Lockhart wondered whom this little pantomime was for.

"Excuse me," he said to the blind man.

"Sir?"

Lockhart watched the blind man turn his head in the direction of the voice, another automatic gesture; empty sunglasses in a dead-white face. The blind man looked like he had never been outside in the daylight. He was about forty, dressed in a golf outfit that did not quite fit him, that wasn't quite clean, and from the relish with which he took up his old-fashioned it seemed that the blind man might drink a little.

"Maybe you can help us out," Lockhart said. "My friend and I were having a discussion . . ."

"Friend?" demanded the blind man. "What friend?"

"Over here," said Margaret.

"Good evening, little lady. Now proceed."

The bartender scowled at all of them and retreated to the far end of the bar. Margaret started to feed pineapple chunks to the dog, who wolfed them down.

"We were talking earlier about whether or not animals have souls," Lockhart said. "Actually, we had it narrowed down to whether or not animals had as much of a soul as humans—so we wouldn't have to figure out if humans had souls."

"Good," the blind man said. "I was going to bring that up."

"And anyway, since you seem to spend quite a bit of time with your canine friend there, I was hoping you might have some thoughts on the matter you could share with us."

"I do," said the blind man, and scooted his barstool six inches closer, the dog following automatically. Margaret was fishing maraschino cherries out of the well across the bar and popping them to the dog, who shagged them easily as Willie Mays.

"My name is Wilson Petie," he said. "After having thought long and hard on this topic for a good many years, I have come to the conclusion that there is no innate difference between the basic existence of myself and the basic existence of that dog, or, God bless her, Trixie, a golden retriever who preceded Rex in this capacity. In other words, that dog is as much of a being as I am or you are."

"Is that all animals?" Margaret asked. "Or just some? How far down the chain of command would you draw the line? Fish? Mosquitoes?"

"Are fish the issue here?"

"They are," Lockhart said. "My friend here claims that it's OK to kill a few fish so the rich vacationers can feel sand between their toes."

"While *he* says it is murder," Margaret said. "All the time he's eating chicken."

She slipped the bone out of a Bong-Bong wing and lobbed the resulting gob of meat toward the German shepherd, who caught it easily.

"I cannot speak to fish," said Wilson Petie. "I cannot speak in regard to fish, I mean. But I will tell you: the fundamental differences between a dog and a human being are in regard to capabilities, not existence. In other words: if you walked on four paws, had a great sense of eyesight and of smell, had fur all over your body and liked to relieve yourself outdoors, you would be—"

"My first husband," Margaret said.

"A dog," said Wilson Petie. "I have felt this through my long years of association with the dog. What I cannot tell you is whether a person would get that same intuition about the inner being of that animal if he or she spent long years of intimacy with a fish."

"So where does that leave us?" Lockhart asked.

"Where we started," Margaret said. "Nowhere. Excuse me, Mr. Petie, but . . ."

"Since birth, eleven months but I had the one before for thirteen years, drive a car."

"What?"

"The three questions you were going to ask," Wilson Petie said, irritably. "How long have I been blind, how long have I had my dog, what's the one thing I'd most like to do—always the same damn three questions."

"Actually, I was going to ask if I could take Rex out into the parking lot and play fetch with him."

"You could drive a car," Lockhart said. "Maybe not solo, but if you had someone to give you some directions and took it nice and easy."

"I've felt the same thing for many years myself," Wilson Petie said. "Unfortunately, I've never found anyone else who agreed with me. How would you like to give me a driving lesson?"

"No problem," Lockhart said. "Come on." He left a ten on the bar and yelled to the bartender to mind their drinks. Wilson Petie groped for the leather handle on the dog's harness and let himself be led out into the parking lot. The night was warm, thick, buzzing with millions of bug wings.

"Now, get yourself situated." Lockhart sat in the back of the Jeep with the dog, Margaret up front, with the top down to get the full rush of wind. "That thing on the left is a brake pedal. You're going to use it when you want to stop . . ."

"I know what a brake does," said the blind man. "I listen to plenty of TV. This must be the gas."

"You got it. Shift lever here." He led Wilson Petie's hand to rest on the shifter between the seats. "Automatic, so you don't have to worry about the clutch. Now we start it up"—he turned the key in the ignition—"and away we go."

They backed up—screeched to a stop—backed some more, almost into a Camaro. Margaret had her hand on the emergency brake, but she waited to apply it, and finally Wilson Petie found the means to stop.

"Easy," Lockhart said. "Nice and easy. Now we'll drop it into Drive."

"This is all right," said Wilson Petie.

Before they started forward, though, Margaret turned and grinned at Lockhart, free and easy. She loves me, she loves me not, she loves me. Lockhart thought, This is it, this is all I've ever wanted. He slipped the gearshift into Lo and the car lurched forward.

"This is all right," Wilson Petie said again. He accelerated forward slowly, listening intently to Margaret's instructions: a little left, left, now straighten it out, that's good, out onto the highway. She leaned forward as he brought it up to speed, intent. Lockhart leaned forward, too, rested his cheek against the side of her head and touched her neck with his hand. The engine roared and heaved in the low gear, propelling them down the dark, deserted lane as slowly and jerkily as a clown-car in a circus. Lockhart felt deranged with happiness.

"I love you," he whispered to Margaret.

"Not now," she said, still poised over the emergency brake.

"This is all right," Wilson Petie said for the third time. In the dashboard light, his face was manic, lit with glee, wind pouring through the sides of the open car.

"Let's go," Lockhart said to the blind man. "Let's do it. Make this pig squeal."

safety

MARIAN IS IN THE BEDROOM, SATURDAY AFTERNOON, TALKING TO
her sister on the telephone, when her two-year-old Will walks
in with a plastic bag over his head.

"Mom," he says, lips muffled by the bag. "Mom!" He seems very pleased with himself.

Then he tries to breathe in, and the thin plastic molds itself to his features, clinging to his face. Will tries to scream. Marian can't seem to move. She can't focus her mind on the problem but thinks instead of how strange it is to see Will's face in a different material, a cast in plastic of his head and shoulders, a something: a bust, she remembers, that's the name for it, and awards herself a little prize for remembering.

But this is no dream. Will takes one step toward her, then runs away, down the hall toward the rest of the house: open doors, branching hallways. She drops the phone and races after him, stopping to look in every open room. Where is he? Where did he go? He's trying to hurt her, trying to punish her for talking on the phone and it's working—she nearly throws up, tasting it at the base of her tongue, a black roaring in her ears, helpless. Her hands dart toward the doors of empty rooms like little panicky animals. Not in his bedroom, not in the guest room, not in the study, not in the kitchen, nowhere—but then in the bathroom, she might see something, the edge of a towel coming to rest.

Finds him shivering behind the laundry hamper. With the nail of her index finger, she slits the plastic where it stretches over his open mouth, and the good air rushes into his lungs, and she feels the convulsions that will bring tears starting deep in his chest. One breath, two, three, he's alive. She tears the bag off his little red face and touches his forehead and his neck, listening for the familiar cries that finally come, ear-piercing.

You little bastard, she thinks. I can't even talk on the phone for one minute . . . This isn't what she's supposed to be feeling, she knows it, and she tries to find the peacefulness inside herself, holding him close, trying to fit inside the memory of the little blue bundle, the milky silences of infancy. But he looks ugly to her with his red, crying face. She can't help it. This is my life, she thinks, this is my only life and you've taken all of it. Before she knows what she is doing, she draws back her open hand and slaps her son across the cheek, not hard.

Marian stops short, not breathing, expecting the world to open under her feet or lightning to strike her down, but nothing happens—only fresh tears from Will, who looks even more blotchy and undesirable than before, but suddenly he's her own child again. She gathers him to her chest and holds him there until the tears subside, whispering, "I'm sorry, I'm sorry, I'm sorry." This is a thing she was never going to do, hitting her child. This is a thing she's not capable of. And her own child, the boy she's given her life to love and protect . . . She searches for the magic saying, the thing that will let her go back and live the last five minutes over again, but it can't be erased. Marian will always know that she hit her child, though Will won't remember long.

Marian is looking over Will's shoulder at the black branches of the trees framed in the bathroom window. It's been snowing off and on for months and the sky is the color of an old nickel. When this winter started she was happily married and maybe she is still. But somewhere out in that cold afternoon is her husband, Robb, who was not here to help when her child almost died. Where is he? At a bookstore. At a bar. Marian can hear her own whiny, bitchy voice, telling Robb, "He almost died! He almost died!" That's it, the bitch voice, the voice he hates, but it's what she feels. What a bitch. No wonder he's gone.

Be fair, she lectures herself. He's only gone to the hardware store. We are happily married. In the front of her mind she repeats the old promises to Will, like a catechism: I will love you, I will take care of you, I will make the world safe for you. Maybe the words will protect him.

That night they leave Will with a sitter and go to the movies and everything's good at first—girls and guns and explosions and loud rock music booming out of the screen—and it's all fine with Marian up to a point. This is Robb's idea of a good time.

Then the girl gets left alone in a big motorboat and the terrorists start burning holes in her with their cigars and Marian checks out. She notices that they are in a place, in a room with three hundred other people. The light of the movie is shining down on the members of the audience and they're laughing or looking scared on cue. They're eating popcorn, holding hands, slouched into their seats. Marian is the only one awake, the only one watching them. It's a kind of power. Robb is laughing along with the rest of them and he doesn't know she's watching him.

After a minute she gets bored with the audience and tries to train her attention back on the screen but it won't stick. People are getting shot and blown up, the girl has a cigar burn on her cheek. Why is this entertainment? But Marian knows why: she likes to see blood, the same as everybody else. Her mother told her, before Will was born, that there was no difference between someone who would hit a child and someone who wouldn't. "You'll never do it," her mother said. "You'll never get there. But you can see how you could be capable of it, even though you never will." Sitting in the theater she re-

106

members how her hands had burned and she could hit him and hit him again and it wouldn't keep him from these stupid things, he was only two years old. You would just keep hitting him and he would never stop crying. Waiting for the movie to be over. It's just nothing she wants to see.

The next day, Sunday afternoon, they bundle up and go to the park, Marian and Will. He plays seesaw with a kid from Laos, feeds the frozen ducks until a dozen cars of men arrive and start to play basketball. "Motherfucker," they shout, every fourth word, "I got you, motherfucker." Their curses hang in the air, suspended in their silvery breath.

When they get home Will takes a nap and the house lapses into quiet, a truce. Robb's reading the last of the paper and drinking the last of the coffee, sitting in the living room, and Marian is allowed into the room only if she will be a good girl. This is Robb's special quiet world. When the telephone rings she fights the urge to apologize.

It's their day-care-person calling to say that Alison, her daughter, is sick with rubella. "Is Will all right?" she asks.

"So far, so good," Marian says.

"You can only get it once," the day-care person says. Her daughter will only be contagious till Wednesday or Thursday, that's what the doctor said. She's sorry for the inconvenience.

"Rubella," Robb says. "Sounds like a blues singer, Rubella Hawkins or something. Little Rubella and the Flames of Rhythm."

"German measles," Marian says. "It's nothing to laugh about."

"I've got a meeting tomorrow that I can't miss," Robb says. "Can you take him? I can maybe take him Tuesday."

"That's all right."

"Wednesday?" And then, when Marian says nothing: "You've got to go to work sometime, don't you?"

"Don't lecture me," she says in her bitch voice. She's instantly sorry but it's too late, the words can't be unsaid, the anger can't be erased from Robb's face. He glowers at her like a parent, as if Marian were a disobedient child too small to punish. A *little* bitch, she thinks. He goes into the living room and starts to read his newspaper again.

If we could only get away for a little while, she thinks, a week or two. If I could have a little break. That would be the practical thing. She sees them on a beach in Florida. It feels like two weeks ago that she was a college student, the endless expanse of days, the luxury of boredom. She remembers smoking a joint with her boyfriend, the last one before Robb, and then bicycling down through the dark Florida streets to get some ice cream. The air smelled like orange blossoms, and she could hear laughter and splashing, the sound of diving, from the backyard pools.

This is just what happens when people get married, Marian tells herself. No bed of roses, as her mother would say. The little things add up. Let's be reasonable. There is the good side. Robb was just brought up to run things, he can't help it—and what's the alternative?

Reasonable Marian. But the little spark of anger won't go out. It's time for her to be good, time for Marian to apologize, but she won't. I'm done praying to the daddy god, she thinks, at least for today. I'm tired of being wrong. And why German measles? There's something heavy, relentless in the name.

Here in the Fatherland. She says, just to hear it, not even a whisper, "My child is very slightly ill with the Italian measles."

"What?" Robb says—pouncing, eager for a clue.

"It's nothing," she says.

The next morning, with Robb gone, she stacks the breakfast dishes into the dishwasher and tidies the empty house. Will is watching television, another small failure. How did she get from her childhood to here? Princess, ballerina. It's snowing again.

She shuts off the TV racket, over Will's protests, though *Sesame Street*'s gone by then and there's nothing on but educational French. They play on the floor: bus, cowboy, house. Will builds a tower as tall as Marian from plastic Duplo blocks—my size, Marian thinks; he can build a thing as tall as me—and a house for the horses, and a house for the alligator. They talk about Eskimos. They lapse into milky, expanded time, clocks replaced by rhythms of hunger, sleep, play, nothing outside the living room. They have Oreos, SpaghettiOs, apple juice, the tap of bare branches on the windows, stray cars splashing by through the slush. They don't need clocks or shoes. They don't need anyone else. This, she thinks, holding him in her lap, sharing a morning snack of bananas and cookies, this right here: a pillow, a comfort, a mom.

By dinner she's tired, by nine worn out. In the lamp-lit quiet of their living room she reads the paper for the first time all day.

"I had a lovely day," she says to Robb. "Alone with Will."

Marian means this as a kind of forgiveness, opening up,

letting him back inside her; she's surprised when Robb doesn't even look up from his magazine, when he gives a sour laugh and shakes his head.

"What's wrong with that?" she asks.

"It's just so childish."

She draws herself back up, then, all the way inside herself, slightly hard to the touch. "Meaning what?" she asks. "He *is* a child, isn't he? He's *our* child."

One of them is going to have to say something. I just want to watch television, she thinks. I just want to live according to the regular clocks of our lives and I don't want you to make words about it. But it's too late. Robb is making up his mind on what to say and then the clocks will all be broken and television won't help. And part of her wants this. Part of her is eager to begin. I will write my name in blood, she thinks, yours or mine, it doesn't matter.

"I don't know," Robb says. "Lately it seems like . . ."

"Sssshhh," Marian whispers, holding up one finger, hearing a faint cry from the top of the stairs. She rushes toward Will, grateful for the interruption, my son, my savior. How did Mary feel, worshipping her son? Women are always praying to somebody. She finds her son sobbing in the darkness of his room. "Tigers," he says, "bad tigers."

"Just a dream," Marian says. In the slit of light from the door, he looks pale, red-eyed, her poor maimed baby. What an ugly child, she thinks, with the tears streaking down his blotchy face. Why can't I shut myself up? She has these feelings and feelings and how can she contain them? She takes her son into her arms as if she could press him back into herself, and rocks him gently as his chest subsides. This is where I belong, she tells herself, this is my rock, the place I touch ground. But she's flying, watching this other mother hold this other child, listening to this other mother whisper, "It's a dream, just a dream. Dreams can't hurt you."

"Bad tigers," Will says.

When he's asleep again she goes downstairs and sits with Robb, with the clocks and magazines. A winter night, pretending to be cozy. Robb has forgotten the near fight, forgotten everything but his own comfort. He's gifted in this way. He'll never know the thoughts in her head, or even whether she has them. Just waiting and waiting until he finally closes his book, clicks off the lamp, kisses the top of her head and goes to bed. Marian sighs with relief, another small luxury. She waits until the bathroom sounds subside and then fifteen minutes more, knowing Robb will be asleep by then. He's a gifted sleeper, too. Marian then pads barefoot into the garage, the oily floor, and collects her down sleeping bag and a couple of foam pads from the camping gear abandoned in the corner.

Am I breaking things? she wonders. The word "survivor" goes through her mind, also the word "rescuer." She thinks of the beautiful quiet of the house today, with the snow falling and Will asleep.

She sets up camp in the night-lit room, next to Will's crib: tucks an extra quilt around him and opens the windows wide to the cold and slides into the slick nylon of her sleeping bag. Her warmth releases the familiar smells of sweat and insect repellent, a specific memory, lying in the beach pines and listening to the waves roll in from the Atlantic, the warm wind rustling in the palm trees, the touch of a boy's naked body next to hers. She shouldn't be here, she belongs in her marriage bed. I shouldn't, I mustn't, I thisn't, I thatn't . . . I vote for warmth and for pleasure, she thinks. Not so much unfaithful to Robb as to this invisible house they have built, their adult lives together. The weight of it, and every day they build a little more.

In the morning they play quietly in Will's room until she's sure Robb is gone.

Still snowing, still quiet. She thinks, I vote for warmth and for pleasure. She makes Will pancakes, not from a mix but from flour, eggs, baking powder, the red Calumet can with the Indian on the front. Wonders what will happen when Robb comes home, if anything will stay unbroken. They line up all the chairs in the dining room and play train, then horsie, a morning of milky quiet. Like music, she thinks: you get the beat and you sing along.

After his nap she decides on an adventure, a trip to the supermarket. This will break the mood. This is the practical thing to do. It's just a mood, a feeling, less substantial than the air. And no wonder: she hasn't put her shoes on for two days, nor has Will, and this far north with the short days it's no wonder . . . She hears the voice of public health. A good brisk walk and you'll snap right out of it.

But getting Will dressed is an hourlong tragedy, and then the slow escape from the house. Money, umbrella, checkbook, driving glasses, extra diapers, snacks, wipes, his little jacket, Byrd left for the North Pole with less. She straps him, finally, into the safety seat in the back of the Volvo and tiptoes out of the garage, armored by all that good Swedish steel. The world outside her living room is dark and small and dangerous. Robb is somewhere out in that world, enjoying himself. The roads are icy and black with water. Filthy snow is piled in the gutters, and all the cars have their lights on in the afternoon, like driving through a tunnel.

In the supermarket no one but Marian hears the music: "If you see me walking down the street . . ." Carts battle in the aisles under the bright lights. Will sits strapped into this folding chair, master of his vessel, hooking random items with his arms and tossing them into the cart: cans of soup, matches, a translucent bottle of Mr. Clean, luminous green, like antifreeze. So many things, so many of each, so brightly colored. I will be like you, Marian says to every passing shopper. This is just what happens when you get married, when you go to live in the Fatherland. What would happen if they just lay down to rest in the aisle? Would the management call the police? Or would they just cordon Marian off with a little blue ribbon, making the other shoppers steer around her, the other mothers courteous, mistaking her for one of their own . . . Marian is rounding one crowded lane when Will reaches out and hooks a half-dozen jars of five-bean salad from a display. In slow motion they tumble over each other, racing to the floor and shattering in bright profusion and glittering shards of glass across the floor.

"Will!" she shouts. "William, you're a bad, bad boy!"

She slaps the soft, exposed skin of his arm. Will starts to wail and then there comes a moment of stillness, like a picture, the other mothers staring, pursing their lips: there's the bitch over there. Some of the other toddlers, captive in their seats, start to whimper along with Will. And this is intolerable. Holding him to her shoulder, she leaves her cart, her coupons, her collected groceries stranded in the middle of the aisle and flees into the dark afternoon. Car, keys, purse, glasses, buckles, nothing simple or clean, no straight lines. Does this happen? Is she the only one? Driving home she sees the eyes of the other mothers, the way they stared at her, and she wants to go back and tell them: I'm under a little stress right now, nothing special. If I could only have a little break . . . At 7-Eleven she buys enough junk to get them through the evening: TV dinners, cheese and crackers, Robb's favorite brand of imported beer. She feels like she has too much money to be shopping here. The clerk is looking at her.

Sesame Street that afternoon is brought to them by the letter "J" and the number "4." Sipping a little white wine, watching Will sing along: it's not easy being green . . . Daytime drinking, another life solution. Robb will come home soon, something will happen. In the one blue eye of the television, dancing shadows on the living room walls, evening fading from the windows, she waits. Will's face is transformed in the television light, enraptured.

"I want to talk with you," Robb says.

She startles at the sound of his voice, looks up to find her husband in the hallway in his green hiking coat, dripping water onto the carpet, a few loose flecks of snow on his shoulders.

She says, "I didn't hear the car."

"I parked it on the street," he says. "I didn't want to block the driveway. I didn't know if you were home or not."

Marian can't read him, can't tell if this is regular hurt feelings or the prelude to something worse, an assault. She goes to him in the hallway, no kisses. She sits on the stairs while he towers over her, the injured party, the daddy god angry at last.

114

"I can't live like this," he says.

"I know."

"I'm worried about you all the time," he says. "Everything is different with you."

She says, "It's just the other day, the suffocation . . ."

"He didn't suffocate. He's fine."

"He nearly did."

"I woke up this morning," Robb says, "and you weren't there and I didn't know where you were."

Tough shit, the bitch voice wants to say. But Marian doesn't even know where the words came from. Whose feelings are these? And Robb is suffering and she's making it worse. His lips are trembling so that his words come out awkwardly, as if his lips disagreed, and she should touch him but she doesn't. Then this silence. Words come and go: I love you, I'm leaving you.

Before she can say a thing, though, she looks past him toward the open door and sees a lovely dark-haired woman in a black raincoat, walking into the halo of light outside their door, slender, ghostly skin, twenty-four or so. She's walking toward their door.

At first Marian doesn't know what to make of this lovely stranger; then realizes, with a choking, slow-motion horror, that Robb has brought a lover home with him—and she's beautiful and she's young, this lover of Robb's, even if she isn't blond. She's the kind of girl who reads books, who could make him happy, who could stand him.

"You really are a bastard, aren't you?" Marian says. "Aren't you a bastard?"

"What are you talking about?" Robb asks. He follows her eyes, turns his back to her just as she starts to shout.

"Get out of here!" Marian yells through the screen. "Just go away."

The beautiful dark-haired woman stops and stares into the dim hallway. "I'm sorry?"

"Shut up!" Robb shouts, looking at something he can see and Marian can't from where she sits.

"What is it?" Marian asks, but Robb pays no attention. He runs to the door and slams the screen open and Will is standing there, dangling at the end of the dark-haired woman's arm. There is Will.

Marian runs to the living room, where she left her son, as if there were suddenly two of him. But his chair is empty, he's not there. She comes back to Will in the hallway.

"I'm sorry," says the dark-haired woman, suddenly awkward. "I saw him in the street. I didn't think you'd want him out there. I mean, I don't mean to interfere, if it's OK with you . . ."

Terrified, Will looks from one face to the next, then sees Marian, too dull to move, stupid as a cow in the hallway, and he dashes past his father and into her arms, and Marian, before Robb comes to take his child away, has a moment when she sees them all from the outside, like a still from some unmemorable film: the beautiful star, standing puzzled in the doorway in her dark hair and glamour, the male lead, earnest, out of his depth, still holding the screen door open, and in the foreground, embarrassing, the sentimental figure of a mother and child embracing.

great falls, 1966

NEEDLES AND NURSE'S AIDES AND LITTLE BOTTLES OF HIS OWN
blood: Evan's been in the hospital for tests three times already,
and he's going back next week. Why won't they tell him?
None of the doctors will say the word "cancer" in his presence

anymore, and his son has used his summer vacation to drive his little family from California. Billy never visits except at Christmas. His kindness is sinister.

The second day after their arrival, Evan talks Billy into an excursion to Glacier Park, though he knows Billy is tired of driving. Kath, Billy's wife, refuses to go. Evan should give up but he can't stand to be around the house with them: they argue, they watch Johnny Carson with the volume way up. And their son: Tim was once his little shining star but now, eleven years old, he is suddenly fat and sullen, a television addict. On the highway he slouches in the backseat, sideways with a comic book, the Incredible Slob Man, according to Evan. Billy fiddles with the radio, jumping without warning from station to station, though it's a mystery how he can hear anything at all over the stuttering roar of the motor. The wind carries a faint stink of burning diesel.

"This car smells funny to me," Evan shouts over the engine. "Are you sure there's nothing wrong with it?"

"This is a perfectly good car. There's nothing wrong with this car."

"Well, I do smell something."

"It's the refineries," Billy says, though they're already miles out of town and the refineries are miles in the other direction. Evan decides to drop it. Better to die here than in the hospital, better quickly than slowly, a fast fiery wreck.

It's hot: the sun shines bright and hard from a ceramic-blue sky, empty of clouds. A simplified landscape, blue above, sunburnt tan and green below, the dusty black asphalt cutting a curve through the hills, two-lane all the way. They putter along at a steady fifty-eight miles an hour, getting passed by everyone. Semi-trucks loom like houses in the rear-view mirrors, waiting for their opportunity, and when they pass, the car shakes like a sick puppy in the side-blast.

At noon exactly—he checks his watch—Billy reaches back into the cooler and opens his first cold beer of the day and his sense of release seems to fill the car. Now there will be a few good hours. Tim leans across the seat back as the mountains break the horizon, and together he and Evan plot their day on a map of the park. The beautiful names: Kintla Peak, Many Glacier, Granite Park, St. Mary. Better here, he thinks, in a place I know. He sees himself sleeping in the dirt of the forest floor, the first soft snows of winter curling over him.

"Let's not get arrested," Evan says. "The police . . ."

Billy scowls at the windshield. "What about the police?"

"Well, they're just watching. You know, behind billboards and all."

"I've never seen a cop behind a billboard in my life," Billy says, "and if we were driving any slower, we'd be going backwards."

Tim is suddenly alert. He leans into the space between the front seats and says, "Let's get a Mustang."

"A gas hog like that—what would we do with it? You just drive from one gas station to the other."

"We could go fast," Tim says. "We could beat all the other cars."

An Indian chief in costume and headdress greets them from the porch of the train station in East Glacier, and for a dollar he lets them take a picture. Evan hands his Instamatic to Billy and stands on one side of the Indian chief, with Tim on the other. Billy fusses with the camera, though there's nothing to adjust. They stand there posing: the fat boy squinting into the sun, the Indian with the grim face of a retired policeman,

119

the weak old man. As Billy goes to snap the lens, a gust of wind comes along and blows Evan's jacket up into his face, surprising him. Evan wants Billy to take another picture, sure he'll look terrible, but Billy's afraid the Indian will want another dollar.

They drive slowly across the Continental Divide, the VW banging and chuffing, cars piling up behind them, working their horns. Half the cars that pass them give Billy the finger, which Evan pretends not to see. The sun shines brightly on the gray rock of the mountains, granite peaks rising out of the forests; like cities, Evan thinks, or the outskirts of heaven. The air is thin, the meadows brilliant Irish green. Evan remembers believing in heaven as a child, thinking this was what it looked like, only warm, inviting.

"Are there bears out there?" Tim asks.

His father waves toward the hills with his open can of beer. "Grizzly bears," he says. "They come down out of the hills every once in a while and eat somebody, don't they?"

"Oh, I suppose," Evan says, abstracted.

"Came down and got one girl right out of her sleeping bag last summer, killed her and then dragged her off into the woods about a hundred yards and ate her leg all the way off."

"All right," Tim says.

"Billy," Evan warns his son, "I don't want you scaring him."

"Are there snakes?" Tim asks.

"Rattlers," Billy says. "Big ones."

Boy talk, Evan thinks, the way it ought to be, and for a moment he almost believes in Billy. He wants to believe, wants to think that all of Billy's thrashing around will someday come to something. Billy teaches fourth-grade science in Stockton,

California, fifteen hundred miles away; he drinks too much, he isn't particularly kind to Tim, he isn't happy. He reaches into the backseat and opens another beer, his fourth, Evan can't help counting. He wants to think that it isn't too late for his son. Too late, too late, too late, the road rushes by, and all the beautiful meadows and the tall peaks and the deep black forests are swept past them in a rush of wind as Evan stares, trying to bring it inside himself. He knows that this is what they will tell him, when they finally tell him: too late, if we could have caught it earlier . . . Give me strength, he prays, and grant me mercy. Already the sun has changed directions, starting its long slant down into the west, where eight or nine hours from now it will set. Two o'clock, and nothing since breakfast.

"I thought we might stop at the lodge," he says. "My treat."

"What lodge?"

"There's one at Lake McDonald," he says, measuring his words. Billy won't want to stop, he drives in a sort of blissful trance, always forward. "I used to go there with your mother, many years ago."

"Sure," Billy says, "whatever you feel like."

This quick acquiescence isn't like him, always pressing onward, believing that if he drives far enough and fast enough, happiness will be waiting for him around some curve. In Billy's easy deferral Evan hears another evidence that he is dying. The word startles him, even as a thought. He wonders what it will be like to say it out loud: I have cancer, I am not going to recover, I am dying. Far below the edge of the road, a lake lies calm and glittering in the sun, nestled into the granite roots of the mountains. What should he have done? This is only scenery, after all, something to look at. But Evan can't help feeling that here is a thing he should have paid attention to.

The lodge is full, tourists from France and Iowa and New York City, teenagers in Bermuda shorts and plaid shirts flirting on the porch, threatening each other with buckets of cold lakewater. There is an Indian chief here, too, or at least a placard explaining who he is and the prices of various things. This Indian chief is apparently on break. The view of the lake is very beautiful, they all comment on it, yet this picture is so familiar to Evan from calendars and postcards and memories that the truth of it comes as a slight shock, a reproach. The cold, indifferent beauty of this place seems like a memory of everything he hasn't done.

After a few minutes' wait in the lobby—wrought-iron furniture and Western prints—the three of them are seated in the back of the big dining room, the picture windows at the far end shining with the famous view, like brilliant Kodachromes. The room is loud with the clatter of glass and china and conversation in different languages. Billy, staring at something across the room, indifferently orders a hamburger and a bottle of beer; Evan asks for a bowl of soup and a glass of water; and Tim orders a meatloaf sandwich and a large Coke.

"Hit the can," Billy says. "Be right back."

Alone, Evan and his grandson stare out the windows, as if something were about to happen. He asks the boy, "Don't you love Montana?"

"Sure," Tim says, eyes left, eyes right, anywhere but meeting his.

"Don't you feel closer to God up here?" Evan asks, knowing he was going too far; but he wants to give the boy something, wants to shake him out of his complacent misery. In a few years he'll be all that's left of Evan—a frightening thought. He says, "I sometimes feel like I'm sitting in God's lap when I'm up here, it's all so clean and pretty."

"We don't go to church anymore," Tim says, eyes left, eyes right.

"You don't have to go to church to believe in God," Evan says. "You don't even have to believe. You can just close your eyes and get that feeling of something all around you." He lets his gaze drift off the boy, out the window, where the mountains are shining in the sun like music, like an opera, he imagines. He says, "There's something special about the mountains, don't you think? Something spiritual. You can see things so much more clearly."

"Dad says you're getting sick."

Tim is staring at him with avid interest, abnormal, as if Evan were a pornographic picture.

"He said I'm not supposed to talk to you about it," Tim says. "He said it's a secret."

Evan's secret. He stares out the window, hoping to find the feeling of a moment before. But there is the view and here he is and they don't have anything to do with each other. Scenery will not solve any of his problems; and at that moment the waitress comes and sets their plates of disgusting food on the table. Evan can't even look at his but Tim digs in.

"What else did your father say?" Evan asks angrily. "What other little secrets did he tell you?"

Tim misses the anger. He pauses between bites to think of what to tell him. Without wiping his mouth, he says, "One of the doctors thinks you're making it up."

One of the doctors, Evan thinks—only one. The rest think I'm gone. But then the thought breaks on him, What if I am?

What if this is only pretend? What if I'm so unreliable that no one should pay attention to me? He thinks of his wife, an argument after a bridge game at a neighbor's house: *You don't even know what you want,* she said, and *It's always the weak ones who screw things up.* Shelley had said the words only once but Evan can still hear them.

"What else did he say?" asks Evan.

"Say about what?" Billy asks. He's returned the wrong way, unseen, unsuspected. Tim tries to disappear without moving, as though, if he sat still enough, he'd change color and blend in with the chair, the tablecloth, his meatloaf sandwich.

But Evan's still upset, a diffuse, floating anger. "We were talking about my illness," he says. "We were talking about how I'm apparently making it all up to get attention."

"That's so inconsiderate," Billy says, with a kind of dreamlike wonder. He takes Tim by the arm and hauls him to his feet, crumbs and meatloaf spilling onto the floor, and slaps him hard across the mouth.

"That's just so inconsiderate," he says again. "That just shows a total lack of consideration for the feelings of others."

The slap seems to still be sounding in the corners of the room—all conversation hushed, all eyes on their table as the red welt starts to blossom around the boy's mouth.

"Excuse me," Evan says, in the silence.

He rises, folds his napkin next to his disgusting soup and leaves the table as the boy starts to weep. The other diners stare as he passes. Don't look at me, he thinks. I did the best I could, always, the best I could.

"Are you all right?" asks the Indian chief. "Would you like to sit down?"

Evan shakes his head, then changes his mind. "Yes," he says. "Yes, I think I would like to sit down."

The Indian chief leads Evan to a slatted Adirondack chair and helps him down, the feathers of his headdress tickling his neck. "A glass of water?" he asks.

"Yes, thank you."

But it's only Evan's mouth that's speaking. Inside he's lit with panic, trying to forget that roomful of people, staring at him, staring at Billy, at Tim. The eyes of other people.

He feels the feathertips against his neck again.

"You want some aspirin or something?" the Indian chief asks, handing him a paper cup of water. "You don't look so hot."

Evan says, "They're going to run over that cooler."

"What?"

"Over there." He points: a family is backing a boat into the water, lowering the trailer down the ramp, but the rear wheels of their station wagon are aimed at their picnic lunch. They're a good-looking family, the mom is anyway, and the three kids—all blond, all having a wonderful time. Evan can't really see the dad, who's driving.

"Hey," says the Indian chief. "Hey, look out!"

They grin at him, and wave.

"No, the cooler," says the Indian chief. "You're going to run right into it."

The family grins again, a little less happily this time, and then the mother calls out a few sentences in a language Evan doesn't understand—Swedish maybe, or German, something with a lot of consonants. Nevertheless her words sound gay to Evan, sounds of greeting, of lighthearted banter.

Just as she is finished saying them, the tires plow into the lunch, shoving the cooler across the asphalt with a horrible grinding sound. The blond family all break out in peals of foreign-sounding laughter.

"Dumb son of a bitch," the Indian chief says.

Evan sips his water. The wind breaks the surface of the lake into coarse ripples, dispelling the reflection of the mountains, but the sun still shines warmly on the water, on the granite peaks, on the weathered brown logs of the porch and on Evan's arms. The mountains are beautiful but, now that nothing else is left, this beauty is terrifying to him, everything he doesn't know, everything he hasn't done. Evan feels enormously tired, afraid to start. He closes his eyes and struggles to open them again. He scans the sky: hours of daylight left, and then the long drive home.

"Tourists," Evan says softly. "They're just tourists. They don't know any better."

blue boy

HIGH ON HIS ALUMINUM STAND, STONED AT TEN-THIRTY IN THE
morning, Kenny studied the day's crop of girls and women
from behind his dark glasses and waited for Mrs. Jordan to
arrive.

The usual moms were spread out with their kids and Garfield towels on the grass next to the patio. They always had this scatter of crap around them, Kenny noticed: toys and clothes and radios and suntan lotion. And the kids were always trying to crawl away and drown themselves. Some of the moms were not bad, the ones who had zipped their bodies back into shape. They wore the sexiest bathing suits so everyone could see their tight little trampoline bellies. Something slightly frightening about them, though, pretending that their kids didn't exist. Something better about the regular moms in the one-piece suits with the weight they couldn't quite hide. Better, Kenny thought, but not sexy.

The other side of the pool, next to the snack bar, was for the girls, the "teens," as they were known around the country club. Teen dances, teen Ping-Pong tournaments. These girls were Kenny's age but that was as far as it went. They saw right through him when they bothered to look at all. Lack of money made him invisible. So he watched them instead, their hard, smooth bodies like car fenders, straight hair and good teeth. They were trying to be sexy but really they weren't and Kenny, staring at them, couldn't figure out why. They lay facedown on their towels on the concrete deck in tiny unstrung bikinis, never moving a muscle, not even lifting their heads to talk to their friends inside the shade of the snack bar. Everybody was friends here, everybody had money except Kenny.

This lifeguard job was a going-away present from his girlfriend. Her dad was on the board of the country club. It was as easy as that. Two days into the summer, everybody figured out that he didn't belong here, Kenny included. He lived in a yellow-brick apartment with his father, near downtown, a thirty-minute bike ride from here. This summer his father had taken to falling asleep on the couch every night with the TV on and a last highball on the floor beside him. Kenny would find him in the morning and cover him up, like a piece of furniture. Some of these girls must have problems, he thought. He wondered what they were, hoped they were serious.

Invisible in his dark sunglasses, part of the patio furniture, Kenny spent his days imagining what it would be like to fuck all the wives and all the daughters of the country club. The only thing they would let him have was skin, and he stole as much of it as he could. He loved to see the pale side of a woman's breast as she lay stretched, top undone, arms over her head, or the pale skin at the edge of her swimsuit bottom, like a promise. He lived for the revealing moment, accidents of skin when a bathing suit was being adjusted or a T-shirt put on, or when a woman would emerge from the water, blind and dripping, and if her suit was made of a certain kind of material, Kenny would see her outlined in every detail, as if she stood naked in front of him. I got you, he thought. Kenny stared and stared.

Not that any of them were possible. Not the girls, not the women. This was just something to do while he was stoned in the big lifeguard chair.

One in particular, though. Her name was Mrs. Jordan and she wasn't a mom and she wasn't a daughter. Every morning at eleven o'clock, when the last shade of the trees was passing from the deck, Mrs. Jordan would arrive alone, press her blond hair into an aqua cap—the exact shade of the blue-tile bottom —and swim fifty laps. Kenny counted, every morning. When she was done she would towel herself carefully dry, then coat herself with sunblock and lie down on one of the lounges, loosening her hair so that it shone different shades of gold and silver in the morning sunlight. Kenny knew it was fake; he wondered sometimes what color her hair was really, but he didn't mind. This was beautiful. This was sexy.

This particular morning she came as usual at eleven and swam her fifty laps and then laid her body carefully down on the chaise lounge. She would stay there, face-down and unmoving, until one-thirty, when she would rise, swim thirty more laps and leave, as she did every day. Every day the same. She lay as still as any of the money kids but she was thinking something, there was something going on inside her head, and Kenny wondered what it was. He made up special stories about her while she lay there. She was waiting to go to prison for drugs, for a long time, and she would be old when she got out. She was dying a slow and painless death, some made-for-TV disease without symptoms, and in her hours on the chaise lounge she was remembering the good years of her life, all spent at poolside. She had time for a last romance, a poolside lover, and Kenny, with his sun-blond hair and his flat, tanned stomach and his vague eyes, would . . .

Suddenly she startled straight upright, looked everywhere, rose to her feet and dove headlong into the deep end of the pool.

This sudden dive filled Kenny with fear: things were happening, things were changing, had he been caught? He looked around the pool and saw only the usual scatter of moms and

130

children and teenage girls; looked into the deep end, following the movement of Mrs. Jordan's dive and saw, tiny and self-contained, bundled into itself, a small child sleeping on the bottom of the water. It can't be sleeping, he thought. It looked so blue through the lapping water, the little bundled child, like an Indian papoose. He watched the broken, refracted line of Mrs. Jordan's body in her black bathing suit.

Before Kenny could move, before he could make up his mind, she was wading out of the shallow end with the drowned child pressed to her chest.

"Jesus!" yelled one of the mothers. "Oh, Jesus, Johnny, what happened to you?" She ran to Mrs. Jordan, screaming, eyes of a wounded horse, while Mrs. Jordan patted the child on the back, as if it had a little cough.

"Johnny!" yelled the mother, ripping him from Mrs. Jordan's arms.

Kenny, who had somehow come to life, took the boy from his mother's arms. He probed the boy's throat, as he had been taught, then laid the blue boy down on a blue-striped towel, tilted his head back, pinched his nose shut and began to try to breathe life back into him. A kiss, he thought, feeling the tiny cold lips against his own. Nothing.

Nothing.

And then, a slow stirring, water boiling out of the boy's lungs, a slow convulsion, then Kenny tasted chlorine, and a gout of water spilled out of the boy's mouth, staining the concrete dark in a spreading pool, and the boy began to breathe again, and he began to sputter and wail. Kenny handed him to his mother. All the money kids were watching, all the moms. The wind was shaking the tops of the trees, showing both the pale undersides of the leaves and the deep green, glossy tops, casting scattered shadows at the edge of the concrete deck. The manager was shouting as he half-ran down the hill from the courts in his hard black shoes, a money kid fluttering behind him.

"Should I call the firemen?" the manager shouted. "Should I call the police?"

"Everything is fine," Mrs. Jordan called out to him, the first words Kenny had ever heard her say. He was startled to hear that she had a Southern accent: Texas? Tennessee? The boy subsided into quiet sobs, pressed against his mother, little pigeon-sounds.

Kenny broke through the circle of watchers and started toward his stand again. His knee hurt deep inside. What did he do to himself? When he looked down it was bleeding freely: he must have banged it on the lifeguard stand, or when he knelt down on the concrete. He couldn't remember how he got from the chair to the boy. There was a slice of time missing. The marijuana haze had left him, and everything was very clear. He sat on a bench near the fence at the deep end and watched them tell their stories to the manager, each in turn, with gestures: headshakes, swooping movements of the hands. In the center of the circle stood Mrs. Jordan, her hair turned dull brown by the water, scattered streaks of fool's gold. She stood flat-footed and troubled in her wet black bathing suit, trying to understand. Her eyes were soft, tired-looking, and the line of her chin was looser than it had once been. Kenny felt his heart pull toward her for reasons he didn't understand. She wasn't perfect anymore. I could hurt her, Kenny thought. I could touch her.

The manager clattered toward him in his black shoes, and the others trailed behind, leaving a group around the mother and child. "What's wrong with your knee?" the manager asked.

"I don't know," Kenny said. "It hurts a little, probably nothing serious." He straightened his leg out experimentally and winced at the grinding inside his kneecap. Something was loose in there.

"Do you want to see a doctor?"

I ought to, Kenny thought, I seem to be damaged. But he couldn't bring himself to ask. He said, "I'm all right, I think."

"Why don't you take today off?" the manager asked. "We can cover for you."

Mrs. Jordan had disappeared somehow.

"Am I in trouble?" Kenny asked.

"I don't know," the manager said. He didn't really want to talk about it. "I don't think so," he finally said. "Why don't you just go home? We'll talk about this tomorrow."

"He saved that boy's life," one of the money kids said, just like she was on television. "That little boy would have died."

"Right, right," the manager said, then turned back to Kenny. "I'm not saying you didn't do the right thing, I'm just, you know, I'm sure you're a little keyed up. We're all a little keyed up. Why don't you go?"

"All right," Kenny said, though when he thought of his father's apartment, he didn't want to go there. The wing of the angel of death has brushed my shoulder, he thought. I don't want to explain to my father.

He felt the eyes of the swimmers on his back as he limped into the locker room. He sat on the bench and looked at his knee, which didn't tell him anything. He was still bleeding from the scraped skin but the real problem was someplace inside where he couldn't see it. He stared at it, waiting for something to happen, but it kept on being his knee, incommunicado. And then he remembered that he had saved a baby's life, and also that he'd almost lost him. Mrs. Jordan, at least, knew he'd almost missed the whole thing. The boy should have died. Who else knew this? But it seemed to matter so little, next to the memory of those cold, tiny lips, the porcelain emptiness of the boy's dead eyes.

In the dim employee's locker room, he showered the chlorine off and changed into his street clothes. He looked around the room and wondered if he would see it again if he was fired. It was a nothing place but Kenny was superstitious about saying good-bye. Too many things in his life—his mother, New Jersey—had disappeared without warning. Good-bye, dead place, unloved rooms. I have fucked your daughters for long enough, or maybe I'll see you tomorrow.

"You're bleeding," Mrs. Jordan said.

"It's nothing much," Kenny said. Then wondered what she was doing there in the driveway of the employee entrance, where his bike was locked to the fence. She wore white loose shorts, a purple top that emphasized her deep, even tan, and tiny gold-strapped sandals. Her hair was nearly dry, beginning to sparkle again. She had a little lipstick on and something to make her eyes look bright and Kenny liked the artifice, though it put her out of reach. Kenny was an inch or two taller but she was looking down at him.

"I think you ought to see a doctor," she said. "I saw you were limping."

"I just banged up my knee a little."

"You don't know what might be going on in there," she said. Her tone implied something reprehensible, a wild party or a Communist cell meeting. She said, "I damaged my knee six years ago from trying to run a marathon and it has never been right since."

"This isn't that bad," Kenny said.

"I didn't feel a thing at the time it happened," Mrs. Jordan said. "Didn't feel a thing."

There didn't seem to be any place for Kenny to put his eyes: he looked down and there were her legs, looked up and there were her breasts under the purple silk and her eyes, which were soft and dangerous. Kenny thought of the dozens of times he had fucked her, and the dozens of ways, and he was ashamed of himself, standing this close. He wanted to escape, wanted to be rid of her.

"I tell you what," he said. "If it still feels bad tomorrow, I'll get to the clinic."

"Rice," she said. "Rest, ice, compression, elevation. The important thing is to ice it down as quickly as you can to keep the swelling down, because the swelling is what does the real damage sometimes. How were you going to get home?"

What did she want from him? Kenny wished he could snap his fingers and she'd be gone, click the heels of his sneakers together three times and poof! He liked her better as a body, a place for him to put his thoughts, but there she was. "I've got my bike," he said.

"Where do you live?" she asked. "How far?"

"Look, I'm going to be fine," he said.

"I'm sorry," Mrs. Jordan said. And for a moment they were the same. It was the blue baby, Kenny thought, remembering how she looked by the side of the pool with her hair down in wet strings and her face naked and worn. He felt a little surge of sympathy for her, though he knew it was misplaced. Adults didn't need his sympathy, at least adults with money. Still there she was.

She said, "I'm sorry, I'm being pushy, aren't I? You go ahead and do whatever you want. I just thought that was a fine thing you did back there and it was like nobody even noticed."

"That's all right."

She shrugged her shoulders. "Well, it bothered me. Sure you don't want a ride home?"

Kenny was about to say no but he thought for a minute: how would he get home otherwise? Maybe there was nothing too wrong with his knee but he wasn't looking forward to riding his bike. And there was this other thing, a vague memory of Mrs. Jordan when she was still in his imagination, before she started to talk, before she turned into an adult. It wasn't much, like a faint perfume. He said, "I guess I could use a ride, if you don't mind."

"I'd be delighted to," she said, smiling, getting her way. He followed her up the gravel drive, shoving his bike. It fit without fuss into the trunk of her Crown Victoria, dark blue with a cream interior. The locks unlocked automatically, the windows all rolled down. Everything was obeying Mrs. Jordan. She swung the big Ford out into the noonday traffic and the cars seemed to part, to make way for her. In her good clean clothes, in her confident driving, she was an adult now, powerful. Kenny felt like what he was: a kid in dirty shorts clutching a Kleenex to his knee. Kiss it, make it better. His own weakness irritated Kenny.

"That blue boy," Mrs. Jordan said, and Kenny knew what she meant, exactly, his smallness and the strange, wrong color of his skin. He seemed so quiet and self-contained. In Kenny's memory, the child sleeping under the water would fit inside a teacup. Then he understood: she wanted to talk it, needed to put it together in her mind. She had held the little cold body too, and the two of them were the only ones who knew.

"What happened back there?" Mrs. Jordan asked. "How did that happen?"

Fuck it, Kenny thought. He said, "I was stoned. I didn't even see him."

"Hmmm," Mrs. Jordan said, then drove calmly onward for a few blocks. Kenny, beside her, was terrified at his own confession. What if she turned him in? The manager wouldn't be happy till he was behind bars. He didn't feel stoned at all, he hadn't since Mrs. Jordan's dive.

"Stoned on what?" she asked at a stoplight, eyes forward.

"Just smoking dope."

"That's not too good of an idea, is it?" A brief glance, enough for him to see she wasn't angry. "This is a disappointment."

"Why?"

She considered a moment. "It's one thing to save a child from circumstance," she said. "It seems like another thing entirely when it's just carelessness, right? I really want to believe that I saved that child's life."

"You did."

"But only from you." She smiled brightly at him, then

pulled away late from the green light. Kenny realized that her words, her manners, were as well thought out and as artificial as her clothes, or her hair. He admired this, too, stuck as he was in sincerity. Brightly, Mrs. Jordan said, "You're bleeding on my upholstery, there."

"Shit," Kenny said, cupping his hand over the wound, wishing away the red-brown stain that had already dried onto the car seat. "Shoot, I mean. I'm sorry."

"No, it's OK, say what you want," Mrs. Jordan said. "You know what I'm going to do?"

Kenny didn't reply but she went on anyway: "I'm going to stop by my house if that's all right, put a bandage on that and then get you some ice. I'm afraid it's going to start to swell up on you if you don't look out. Is that OK?"

"Sure," Kenny said, dirty jokes running through his head, *Playboy* cartoons about grocery boys. What did she have in mind? Nothing, he knew: she was doing him a favor and nothing more. But he couldn't be sure. There was always that other possibility and she looked fine driving down the avenue with her hair all gold again. Mrs. Jordan was sort of coming and going, fading in and out. Kenny found himself looking at the outside of another person, wondering what was going on inside that skin. What was it like to be Mrs. Jordan, what was she thinking? Or: what did she do when she was "thinking"? Was it the same thing that Kenny did, or was it another thing altogether? Kenny thought of the inside of his own mind as a small deserted island, well-worn paths through the tired bushes. The mental landscape of Mrs. Jordan, on the other hand, he imagined as dense with foliage and flowers, a perfumed jungle roamed by wild and dangerous animals, bright eyes glittering elusively.

"Here we are," she said, pulling the Crown Victoria into the drive of a big bland colonial, an exploded dollhouse. As they crawled up the blinding white clean concrete driveway, the garage door rolled obediently open, into the gasoline darkness, and then shut again behind them.

"Would you like a lemonade, or a Coke, or a cup of coffee? We have everything," she said. "Would you like a beer?"

A beer, he thought immediately, something to calm him down. But he lacked the nerve. "Iced tea, if you have any."

"We do," she said. "Of course we do."

She left him bleeding in the backyard, an even carpet of green punctuated by flowering shrubs, like covered chairs. Beyond the yard rose the edge of a deep, tangled forest. No one could see in, they couldn't see out. Dappled sunlight, a cool intermittent breeze. Kenny knew this place in dreams: the place of no excuses, no explanations. Everything was perfect. In a moment Mrs. Jordan would come out barefoot and she would stand at the edge of the grass and take her earrings off and then loosen her white shorts and let them fall to the grass and she would step gracefully out of them. Or she would call to him from the upstairs bedroom. Or he would be walking down a hallway, for some reason he couldn't figure out, and accidentally see her through a half-open door, half-naked, changing out of her damp bathing suit, and she would look up and see that he caught her and look at him with that same open look he had seen at the poolside and then she would open the door and take him by the hand, her own hand still damp from the bathing suit, the white flesh where the sun didn't reach . . . Kenny wondered: where does the shit in my head come from?

"Lemonade," said Mrs. Jordan, and poured him a glass, though he seemed to remember that he'd asked for something different. Next to the pitcher of lemonade she set a metal roll of adhesive tape and a couple of gauze pads in aromatic waxy envelopes that smelled like Band-Aids, that made him feel like a small child again.

"I'm terrible at first aid," Mrs. Jordan said. "I'll try my best but I flunked my merit badge, I'm afraid."

The fragrance of Band-Aids: Kenny remembered an ordinary afternoon, home from school, contagious but not really sick, eight years old, ears buzzing with fever, reading at the kitchen table—reading a Superman comic book, with Mr. MX-YZPTLK as the villain—and his mother boiling hot dogs for their lunch and his father calling, some trivial reminder, and his mother hanging up the phone and sitting silently at the table for a moment, raging, and then standing up and dashing the pan of hot dogs against the wall, splattering the kitchen with boiling water, burning her own hand badly—he remembered the scarlet stretched-tight texture of her skin as she rubbed butter into the burn, not looking at him. Kenny was unhurt, a few tiny droplets landing on the skin of his arm, in places he could still feel: there and there and there. The opposite of this orderly, sunlit yard. I'm not one of you, he thought, looking at Mrs. Jordan's golden head.

"All done," she said. A spotless square of gauze was fastened to his leg with tidy strips of tape, a haze of antiseptic school-nurse aroma. "All better," she said.

"Thank you," he said, trying to will his attention away from her body. But he had fucked her so many times in his thoughts that it was hard to stop, and she wasn't wearing much, and she was right there.

"It wasn't that bad to start with," she said. "Jesus, I can't stop thinking about it."

"What?"

"That boy, the way he almost drowned." She eased into a chair, across the glass-topped table from him, and stared off into the woods at the edge of the lawn, thinking. Kenny stole intimate glances of her body while she was unaware. Assuming she was unaware.

She said, "It's just so many million-to-one shots: if I hadn't happened to look, if you hadn't known how to do that breathing thing, if he'd been down there a minute longer. It makes you wonder how anything ever happens at all."

"It makes me wonder why his mother wasn't watching him," Kenny said.

"Or the lifeguard, Kenny," she said, with a little cold smile.

"How did you know that?"

"What?"

"My name? How did you know my name?"

"I don't know," she said. "I heard it at the club, I suppose, or you told me. Why? What's so strange about that?"

"Well, I don't know yours," he said, a little amazed at his own audacity, fearful. He was asking for more than a name. Mrs. Jordan seemed to know this, too; she hesitated for a moment before answering.

"Linda," she said. "Linda Lavinia Jordan. I'm very pleased to meet you." She extended her hand across the table, formally, and Kenny shook it. Her hand was small, soft, vaguely perfumed.

"Lavinia?" he asked.

"After an aunt," she said. She seemed to have explained this many times before. "Everybody's got to have some kind of middle name. What's yours?"

"Milton," he said ashamedly. "Kenneth Milton Kolodny. My mother was an English teacher."

"Was?" asked Mrs. Jordan. "She's passed away?"

"Oh, no," Kenny said, then found that he couldn't go on. His mother was in the hospital, on that day, at that hour while Kenny sat enjoying his lemonade in the clear light of Mrs. Jordan's patio. He thought of the hallways more than anything else, pale green linoleum, smells of rubbing alcohol and old clothes and vomit. Where she was likely to remain. The man in the next room would scream as if he were being murdered, any hour of the day or night. Kenny felt like an imposter, like any words he cared to say would be a lie, anything but the unsayable truth: I am the son of people in trouble, I carry this sickness with me.

"It's all right," Mrs. Jordan said, looking at him curiously. "I shouldn't have asked."

"It's complicated," Kenny said. He felt the distance between them again, two lives, two silences. At the same time, he felt an obscure victory: this confusion was at least his own, it was something Mrs. Jordan couldn't know. It was one thing he was better at. For the first time since he had breathed the boy back to life, Kenny felt that he had his own shape, a person after all. He was learning something here. At least his problems were his own.

"We should get going," Mrs. Jordan said. "I have some errands to run this afternoon, and I'm sure you need to get going. You're all fixed up." She didn't seem anxious to go, though. Her drink was only half-finished, she stayed in her chair. Kenny wanted to ask her why she had brought him here, though he suspected there was nothing like a reason. He imagined himself moving to touch her, standing behind her chair and letting his hand caress the soft skin of her neck, her shoulders, while she bent her head to welcome him.

She said, "That was a remarkable thing today, wasn't it?"

"That was amazing," he said. "You were amazing."

"It wasn't much," she said, ducking her head, pleased. "I just don't know how I managed to see him. I don't know what made me look up."

"You were awake?"

"Oh yes," she said, "I'm always awake."

The questions sprang to his mind but he didn't dare ask them: What are you thinking? What are you doing? He saw her on the chaise lounge, every curve of her gold bathing suit, every line of skin, like a photograph in front of him. The face that was turned toward him now seemed superimposed on that memory, so that he saw two sides of her at once. How many Mrs. Jordans?

"A remarkable thing," she said again, softly, like a door closing. Then, in a sudden burst of energy, she drained her drink and assembled everything onto the tray again: tape, scissors, disinfectant, lemonade. "Time to get going," she said, rising. "But thanks for coming by. I'm going to remember this day, I think."

"Me, too," Kenny said, following her into the bland interior of her house, sofas and coasters and pictures of relatives in elaborate frames. Purse, telephone, refrigerator.

"I'll be back in a second," she said, and disappeared upstairs.

Kenny stood in the kitchen door, next to the winter coats, men's and women's woolen overcoats hanging on their pegs like abandoned persons. In the dead of summer these coats seemed exotic as sponge divers' outfits. There was a man's good gray overcoat hanging on the rack, a husband's coat. Kenny felt an obscure jealousy, as if he were married to Mrs. Jordan, as if the child sleeping under the water had been their own child, born into the air again. On an impulse, Kenny put his hand into the pocket of the overcoat, a soft, solid pocket meant for a bigger hand than his, and brought out a passcard for the Washington subway, a white cotton handkerchief, a scrap of gum wrapper and seven dollars, two singles and a five. Kenny kept the money and the passcard and stuffed the handkerchief back into the coat pocket, the yellow gum wrapper fluttering to the floor in his hurry. Now this ordinary hallway felt dangerous, as if it had suddenly been raised fifty feet off the ground, so that walking it required care. Kenny didn't know why he had taken the money. He wasn't a thief. The money was part of something that belonged to him. He wasn't stealing so much as taking his own back. Mine, mine, mine.

"All set?" asked Mrs. Jordan, sweeping into the room, bending by the coats to pick up the yellow, guilty scrap of gum wrapper. Kenny felt his throat close, certain he was caught, but she only dropped it carelessly into the wastebasket. She held the door to the garage open for him, then locked it behind her while he stood in the half-lit darkness, not sure what to do with himself. The motor of Mrs. Jordan's big Ford was ticking as it cooled. The stolen money felt hot in his pocket and he was getting away with it and he knew something that he didn't know before: that all you had to do was reach out your hand and try for it. Kenny fell out of his childhood in an instant, as soon as he saw that all the rules and all the things you were supposed to do were made-up things for children. That was what his father knew, and Mrs. Jordan, and now Kenny: that you just did what you wanted, you opened your hand and tried to grab for it and the rules didn't matter.

"Linda," he said.

She turned away from the door and stood uncertainly, as if she were trying to remember something, put something together. She was standing maybe two feet away from him, cans of ancient paint and weed killer and hose attachments on the shelves behind her. The bare skin of her arms, the curve of her neck. Kenny stretched his hand toward her and touched behind her neck.

He raised his eyes to her face and knew at once that he had mistaken her. Surprise, then fear, crossed her face as she edged away from him. "What are you doing?" Mrs. Jordan said, stepping back away from him. "What did you think . . ."

Her mouth was open, she couldn't understand. In an instant Kenny moved from inside to outside, a camera zooming out too fast. He saw who they were, where they were: a boy, a woman, a Ford. He saw the fear plainly on her face and thought, for the second time that day, I could hurt you. I could fuck you if I wanted to. She was trying to unlock the car but she kept looking back at him and she couldn't find the lock with her hand and he understood that he had the power if he wanted it.

"I don't mean to hurt you," he said.

But this only made her more scared, scared of Kenny. He could see it in her face as she backed toward the car, trying to make herself small, invisible. And Kenny thought, if that's the way you want it. He didn't have the thought for long, just for a second, but it was long enough to remember, long enough so he couldn't deny it: if I can't get it any other way, I'll just take it. As long as I'm nothing now, nothing but a fear, I'll just take it. And this was the thing that scared him, that made him drop his arms to his sides and walk backward away from her toward the kitchen door. "I'm sorry," he said. "I didn't mean anything by it."

"That's all right but it's time for you to go," she said quickly, not looking at him. She got the car door open and then the garage door was rising up by itself and the daylight came flooding into the spidery darkness and it was gone. She was starting the car.

"Wait a minute," Kenny said. "My bike. It's in the trunk."

She looked up at him, suspicious, wondering if this was a trick. Then she put the car into reverse and for a moment Kenny thought she was driving away with his bike; she backed the big car out of the garage and into the street and turned. Then she stopped the car and got out and opened the trunk and got back into the car before Kenny could reach her. He heard the garage door rolling shut behind him as he wrestled the ten-speed out of the trunk. When he slammed it shut she was driving away instantly, around the corner and gone, leaving him alone with his bike on the street of big blank houses. He tried to pedal the bike but it was no use with his bad knee—the bandage got in the way and the gravel inside was burning and grinding. He turned back for one last look at Mrs. Jordan's big white house shining in the sunlight. It was a house without a face, without an expression. You couldn't even tell if anyone was home or not. All the houses on this street. He felt like they were staring at him as he started for home, pushing his bike, limping down the asphalt on his swelling, bleeding knee.

Smoking cigarettes on the porch in the cool night, the river sound of traffic on the avenue two blocks away, Kenny watched the streetlight shadows on the sidewalk. Taxis and cats. The smoke curling out into the light from under the eaves of the porch gave his eyes something to rest on. Kenny loved to smoke, but usually he didn't let himself. He had drunk two of his father's Ballantines, had thought about drinking four or five more—he wouldn't get in trouble for it—but being drunk would only fill him with big useless emotions. Kenny had learned that much from his father.

If I can't get it any other way, I'll just take it. Her face in the light of the one bulb in the garage, the fear on it, over and over.

Kenny heard his father whistling before he saw him, "Sentimental Journey" from a block away. A little after two, closing time at the Moon Palace, the only tolerable bar in walking distance according to Kenny's father. He was an expert whistler, a virtuoso. The plain melody of the song was broken and turned inside out, embellished with trilling melodic runs and odd accents, derived, Kenny knew, from the show-off jazz pianists his father loved, Art Tatum especially. He seemed to be walking all right. He hauled himself into one of the porch chairs and took a deep breath of the night air, shaking his head. Then turned to Kenny. "Get me a beer, would you?"

Kenny hesitated. Normally he wouldn't, not when his father was already drunk, they both knew that, but this was a day when all regular bets had been canceled. "For Christ sake, Kenny," his father said. "Just a beer, OK?"

Kenny fetched the beer for him. Though he wanted one himself, he decided against it, not wanting to go along with his father. Not wanting to be his father's son, he got himself a glass of water. The beer could wait; his father wouldn't last long. He was smoking one of Kenny's cigarettes when Kenny came outside again.

"Did you hear about this Miss America thing?" his father asked. "They caught her, I guess she was in one of these dirty magazines fooling around with another girl, I mean, Jesus. Everybody's cheating." He stubbed his cigarette out and lit another from Kenny's pack. "People cheat on their taxes," he said, "people cheat on their marriages. Everybody wants something for nothing, you ever think of that?"

It occurred to Kenny that the cigarette his father was smoking was bought with one of the dollars he'd stolen from Mrs. Jordan's house. An intricate balance of right and wrong and just plain taking. You wanted something and you reached your hand out and took it. Kenny knew he had learned something that day he would not forget.

"Don't ever go to law school," his father said, and settled back into the chair.

There was nothing Kenny wanted to talk about with his father. He didn't even know how he would put it into words: I saved a life today and then something happened . . . Something was taking shape inside him, his own life, his own life story. He felt restless, ready to move on, but he knew that his life would burst out of him when the time came, and not before. Still, he was restless, restless.

"That was really something," the manager said. "You saved that boy's life."

Kenny wished he would go away. The night before had never quite ended, the day felt stillborn, hot and sluggish. His knee was swollen and bruise-purple and it hurt. The money kids gathered, as if around an accident. The manager said, "The board would like to give you this, and also to thank you for a tremendous service."

He beamed at Kenny and offered his big hand, like congratulating a banjo, and the money kids broke into fake applause. Kenny smiled until they all went away, then climbed his chair to watch the morning sun crawl across the deck and wait for Mrs. Jordan. After a while it occurred to him to open the envelope that the manager had pressed into his hand, where he found a check from the club for twenty-five dollars, which seemed like the exact wrong sum of money. It should have been more or it should have been nothing.

The blue baby, he thought, the image already fading from his mind, like the sample photographs in drugstore windows, smiling faces disappearing into monochromatic blue. Our child. Nothing had really happened, it was just a misunderstanding. The waiting was killing him. The minutes before eleven o'clock, when Mrs. Jordan would or wouldn't come, when she would or wouldn't ask to speak to the manager, the minutes crept by like palsied old men. Something needed to happen. Wreckage would suit him as well as anything else. He wanted some definite action, some release, that moment when the wave takes and tumbles you underwater and you either come up into the air or you don't, but this day seemed stuck in a perpetual sunlit middle. Two teenage girls reclining on silvery air-mattresses, the smell of cocoa butter, the snack bar radio playing stale sixties hits: "My Guy," "Crosstown Traffic," "Ride My See-Saw."

Eleven came and went without her.

She could not do this to him. If she was at the manager's office, fine, if she was at the police station, if her husband—if she had a husband—was on his way down to the club. But to leave him like this, in between, Kenny would split open and spill his insides on the clean cement of the deck. This nothing.

A few minutes later, though, a few minutes late, she came out of the women's changing room in her usual suit and her usual sandals. She swam her usual fifty laps and then arranged herself, without a word to Kenny or a look at him, on the usual chaise lounge and began to do whatever she did, which Kenny would never know. No managers, no police, no husbands. Things were just going on. Kenny's mother was alive, his father, Mrs. Jordan was alive. Instead, this emptiness inside him, growing to fill his skin. The sunlight seemed hollow, slanting down on the empty patio, slanting toward September. From behind his dark glasses he stared down at Mrs. Jordan, her legs, her hips, the lovely line of her arms, her hair that sparkled artificial gold and silver in the sun. Useless anger boiled inside his chest. There were still six weeks of summer left.

a stranger in this world

HER HUSBAND IS STANDING IN FRONT OF THE BATHROOM MIRROR, shaving. He has just taken a shower, and the glass is all steamed up except for a patch where he's wiped it clear with his hand. Greg is naked but easy, not stiff and awkward, the way most men get when they know they're being watched. He's still twenty, the age he will always be. And Candy is also naked, except for a pair of shoes, and she's also still twenty. They're dressing for a party or for dinner out, something fancy. He catches her reflection in the mirror and looks at her sternly, like a father. Candy asks him, "Do you like my outfit?"

"With shoes like that, you don't need an outfit," he says, and continues to shave. Candy embraces him from behind, and her shoes have made her tall: she can see over his shoulder. She can feel his soft, damp skin with her hands. She tries to remember what kind of shoes she has on, but she can't remember and it doesn't matter now. There's a strange feeling in her body: it's almost like she has a penis. She can feel it rising, getting hard against Greg's backside as he continues to shave. It's a strange feeling but familiar, as if she's had a penis all her life but forgotten it. How could she forget such a thing? The wind is rising next to her head . . .

The wind was rising next to her head and Walter was saying, "I'm sorry, I'm sorry."

Candy took a moment to realize that she'd been dreaming —and even then, the flavor of the dream persisted, stronger than the real thing. She turned to Walter, her boyfriend, and said, "What?"

"We need to figure it out, what we're doing," Walter said.

Candy sat up, straightening out her shoulders and her neck, which had a crick in it from sleeping on the car seat. She could still feel Greg's skin on her hands, but outside the window the Smoky Mountains were rolling by at sixty miles an hour. "How long was I out?" she asked him.

"A couple of hours," Walter said. "Since Asheville, anyway. You slept through the best part."

"Little do you know," Candy said. She lit a cigarette and put her knees up on the dash and watched the scenery unwind. When she turned up the radio the Reverend Al Green came through the speakers, Jesus will fix it, which seemed about right. She felt the countryside calling her out of the dream, felt the allure of driving: movement, freedom, scenery. They were coming out of the mountains on a wide, empty white concrete highway, warm in the afternoon sun. Where the hills had been left alone, they were covered with green forest, the hundred different greens of spring. Where the highway cut through, or where developers had leveled the ground for a supermarket or a tire store, the earth showed through as a wounded red. Sometimes the road would curve up next to the woods and she'd look into the darkness to see the wild dogwoods deep inside, white flowers shaking in the wind like escaping deer.

"What's this decision of which you spoke?" she asked him. "Which you disturbed my slumbers for."

"Well, it's getting late and I was thinking—we can stop now, get a motel for tonight, or else we can just keep going."

"How far?"

"I don't know, seven or eight hours," Walter said. "There's all of Georgia still to go."

"And miles to go before I sleep," she said, "and miles to go before I sleep." She stared out the window at the passing forest, unfocused her eyes so it became a green blur. She wished she were back inside her dream, safe with her husband, who had been dead for twelve years, killed in a plane wreck on the runway in Izmir, Turkey. He was a fighter pilot. Walter was a boyfriend. When do they stop being boyfriends? she wondered. Candy was thirty-four years old and she still had a boyfriend.

"Maybe we should just skip it," she said.

"What do you mean?"

"I've got a college friend in Sarasota, she lives on the beach." With her husband and three kids, Candy remembered suddenly, but still it might be better than Walter's parents.

"I already told them I was coming," Walter said. "There's no escape for me. I can drop you at the bus station if you want."

"Do they think we're getting married?"

"I have no idea what they think. I mean, that's why I moved fifteen hundred miles away from them."

Candy thought wistfully of the white-sand beaches of Sarasota, spring sunshine and college boys with ladders of muscle up their abdomens. She said, "Let's just keep going, I guess."

"If that's what you want to do. I don't know why you're in such a hurry to meet my mother. I wouldn't be, if I were you."

"Well," she said, "you know, firing squad. Get it over with."

"You don't know, Candy, you just don't know." He sounded like he was scolding her, like a husband, or a father, and for that moment she hated him. It wasn't fair, he didn't mean anything by it, but she hated him. He was so even-tempered, he knew so much, he was so reasonable and rational and good with his hands that she hated him. In contrition, Candy scooted toward Walter, across the bench seat of the Impala, and leaned up next to him like a high school girl. She turned the radio up again and the Gospel Harmonettes of the Full Zion Baptist Church of Durham, North Carolina, were singing "He Gives Me Strength." Walter put his arm around her and tapped his fingers on the wheel in time to the beat of

154

the choir. She slipped her hand between his open legs, aligning her fingers with the inside seam of his jeans.

"What's this called?" she asked him. "I see couples sitting up close like this. Is there a name for it?"

"Riding bitch," Walter said.

The song on the radio dissolved into a ruckus of singing and shouting and applause—Praise God! Can I praise his name?—and then the next began to take shape out of a few spare piano chords.

"Riding bitch," Candy said, tasting the words in her mouth. Bitch. "If they sounded like that in my church, I'd still be going on my own."

"No, you wouldn't," Walter said, letting his hand idle down her shoulder so it rested on the top curve of her breast. "I'm sorry, Candy, but you wouldn't be caught dead in church if they didn't pay you."

"OK, OK, OK, OK," she said, not wanting to argue, preferring her thoughts to his company. She felt an invitation in the white flowering dogwoods to go follow them, a fairy-tale beginning, adventures in the greenwood. She closed her eyes and felt the wind on her face. The lead singer for the Gospel Harmonettes was shouting, in a high clear voice, that she was nothing but a stranger in this world.

Walter's family's house: pink speckled brick, with columns across the front. It sat alone on a naked dirt hillside like a billboard, caught in a pool of floodlights. It looked like it was about six weeks old and about an inch thick, propped up with two-by-fours at the back. What was she expecting? The

Legendary South, the Romantic: moss and rot; white-washed cypress porches; a spreading live oak in the yard; in the living room, maroon velvet fading to brown. But this thing looked like part of a Barbie set, new, cheap and pink. Even the landscaping looked fake, stiff little bushes and a green felt lawn, stolen from a model railroad.

The mother was worse: handsome, well-preserved, with teeth like the keys of a child's piano. She came to greet them at midnight in full makeup and peach satin pajamas, clutching her robe around her to ward off the chill of the house. It was still ninety degrees outside. She spoke so slowly that Candy found herself finishing the thought before Walter's mother could finish the sentence:

You must be . . .

It's so good . . .

I've heard so much . . .

It's terrible of Walter to make you drive . . .

Kabuki: things were being communicated, nuances of meaning between mother and son that Candy couldn't grasp. Things were being said about her. What?

"I've put you in your old room," Walter's mother told him, "and I've put your friend in the spare room at the top of the stairs."

"Why not the guest room?"

"Well," his mother said, "I'll leave you to work that out with your brother. I guess that he and Kaye have been having a little bit of a spat—he's been camped out in the guest room for a couple of weeks now. You're welcome to try to dynamite him out."

Suddenly, disconcertingly, she turned her eyes on Candy.

"He stays up all hours," she said. "Walter tells me you're a late riser, too."

She tilted her head like a curious bird, waiting for a response, Candy couldn't imagine what.

Then back to her son. "The early bird catches the worm," she said, "and at my age I need all the worms I can get. I'll leave you two to work out the sleeping arrangements with Jimbo. It's wonderful to see you, sweetheart."

She embraced her son and went off, never again noticing Candy. "Let's get ourselves something to drink," she said. "I can still feel the road, like I'm vibrating or something."

"It is so strange to be back here," Walter said. "Especially with you here, and all."

Candy followed him, wondering exactly what the hell he meant. They went through the mahogany darkness of the dining room, through hallways lined in soft beige carpet, absolutely clean, with a smell of pine air freshener. It was the kind of house that made her want to smoke cigarettes and spill the ashes. The kitchen at the back of the house was as clean and tidy as an operating room, and there at the kitchen table was her husband.

It was Greg.

Except that it wasn't Greg, the second time she looked, but a man who was the same size, tall but solidly built, a man with the same dark military hair and the same long hands and something else—some way of moving or of holding his body. When she took the feeling apart this way it started to disappear, but when she just looked at him it came flooding back again and she was having a bright moment, the way a perfume she hadn't smelled in a dozen years would spin her back in time, like a sudden hole in the floor. Not-Greg was tipped back in a wrought-iron chair, watching a little black-and-white TV on the glass-topped table in front of him, Barbara Bain, Martin Landau—*Mission: Impossible.* Next to the television was a square bottle of Early Times bourbon and an ice bucket in the shape of a diver's helmet that was larger than the television. The glass was in his hand, in Greg's hand.

Candy knew it was a mistake but she couldn't stop her heart from leaping toward him. The secret hopes that had stalked her, always—he'd ejected somehow; he'd been living in the jungle; it was all part of a secret government plan—all came true at once, all came out of the darkness and into the light of her mind. It was Greg, he was alive, their happiness could begin again. Then he turned toward her with the slow quizzical movements of the politely drunk.

"Walter," he said. "I seem to be bothering your friend here. Why don't you introduce us?"

"Candy Collins," Candy said, walking toward him, giving him her hand. She let it rest in his for a moment too long, loving the familiar warmth of his hand, the way they fit, hand in glove. This is not appropriate, she thought. This man is not my husband.

"James Madison," said Walter's brother, "like the President, some very distant relation of ours according to our mother."

"Who made it up," Walter said.

"Who made it up," agreed his brother. "You can call me Jim like everybody else. I think Mr. President would be excessive, don't you?"

"I kind of like it," Candy said.

"Whatever you want," Jim said. "Are you a spy like Walter here?"

"I'm a translator," Walter said.

"What have you been working on lately?" Jim asked, and both the brothers grinned at each other. Jim turned to Candy and said, "Exhibit A: he can't tell us. He's a spy, I'm warning you. Or maybe you're a spook, too?"

This man is not my husband, Candy thought, and dreams can't make him so. But it was lovely to look at him, lovely to pretend, and these were questions he would be asking if he came back: Who have you become? What have you done with yourself? It took her a minute to gather her answers into a small enough package. "I work in a bookstore," she said.

"And she's a singer," Walter said, advertising her—and in that moment of promotion she saw the balance between them, Walter the younger brother trying to catch up with Jim the older, who would always be out ahead of him. And this was sad, this endless game of catch-up, except that Candy realized then that she didn't care what happened to Walter, not at all. Not by comparison anyway.

"What kind of singer?" Jim asked, and Candy felt herself blushing.

"Lately I just sing in a church choir, every Sunday. They pay me." This wasn't enough, and Jim waited for more until she said, "I started out to sing in the opera."

"I thought opera singers weren't supposed to smoke cigarettes," Jim said.

"Well, I'm not going to sing in the opera, not now. I'm not quite good enough."

"She's got a beautiful voice," Walter said. Jim looked over

at him as if he suspected Walter was lying, and Walter said, "She does!"

"It's like a trick," Candy said, and she was talking directly through Jim and straight to Greg, wherever he was, explaining herself. "It's like you work and work to develop your voice, and after a while it's not even part of you anymore, it's just this thing that lives in your throat. And you have to take care of it, and look out for its moods, and so on. And then you can sort of hear it sometimes, and then one day you just realize: not quite."

The brothers looked at her like she had grown antennae out of her forehead. Then Jim said, "Let's hear it."

"I don't want to wake everybody up."

"We can go outside."

"I want a drink first."

Jim didn't reply but grabbed the bottle of Early Times off the table and waved it at her and led them out the back door, Walter stopping along the way to get a can of beer from the refrigerator. Outside was blood-warm, bathtub-warm, ten million bugs off in the night. The green grass of the yard ended as abruptly as the edge of a rug, at a barbwire fence about thirty feet from the back door. Past the fence were a tree and a cow and the shadows of the other cows moving around in the darkness. The brothers arranged themselves around the picnic table and looked up at the stars. This is the life, they were telling her. This is the real thing, burbling whiskey from the bottle.

Candy lit a cigarette, sweat prickling on her skin from the nearness of Jim, and she was getting close to a place that was past pretending. There was a real thing called love and she had forgotten it, what it was like to say his name, to touch his back in the middle of the night, to lace her fingers through the short

160

hairs at the back of his neck, pressing his head closer while he kissed the nipples of her breasts. She felt a trembling that started in her ovaries and spread throughout her body. She took the whiskey bottle from Jim's hand and drank, a sacrament. Then started to sing: *Amazing Grace, how sweet the sound, to save a wretch like me . . .*

"That's beautiful singing," Jim broke in, "but that song, I don't know, maybe a little depressing."

"That's a beautiful song," Walter said, and he looked toward Candy for approval. But she didn't care about him at all. She was looking straight at Jim, and all of them saw.

"What would you like to hear?" she asked him.

"Sing the blues," Jim said.

"I thought you didn't like depressing music."

"That Jesus shit is depressing," Jim said. "The blues is a sweet thing, isn't it?"

Neither of the others replied. Candy was trying to sort out where he was serious and where he was mocking, feeling the conversational sand shift out from under her feet—and she wanted him to admire her, wanted him to dream at night of how cool she was. More than anything she wanted to tell him where she was, not the body that anyone could see or the mess that she had made of her life but the tiny soul that was somewhere inside. All around her in the night, the bugs and birds were saying the same thing: I'm here, I'm here, I'm here . . . Come find me, come and meet me in the dark fields.

She sang "Lover Man," as dark and bittersweet as she could. The usual thing when she was singing, her voice felt bigger than she was and after a minute she wasn't there anymore and it was only the voice and the song, the music dissipating in the damp night air, the apathetic stare of the cows.

She liked herself best when she was almost nothing, slowly reassembling herself when the last notes had escaped her, feeling like she'd gone too far: Lover man, where can you be?

"Not bad," Jim said. "A little stiff, but you're good for a white girl."

But he was being complimentary, and Walter was staring at her, and Candy had made some little mistake, some tiny mistake, and this was not going to amount to anything either, this evening or this trip. Or this lifetime, she thought, bowing to herself like Sarah Bernhardt. My tragedy, yeah, yeah, yeah. She looked at Jim, who didn't look like a husband at the moment, hers or anybody else's. "Excuse me," she said. "I have this headache kind of thing. From the driving, I guess."

"Two aspirin and a drink of whiskey," Jim said. "It works for me, sooner or later."

But he was showing off. The boys were disappointed because their audience was leaving, and it was no fun to practice alone, and Candy made up her mind. "I think I'll just get some sleep," she said. "I'll be all right in the morning."

"I'll take you up," Walter said.

"Sleep tight," Jim said. He stayed outside with the whiskey bottle, listening to the bugs, looking at all the stars: I'm here, I'm here, I'm here . . .

Walter led her around the house to the front again and it was like starting over. He fetched their suitcases from the trunk of the Impala, humped them over the threshold and up the staircase to the darkness at the top of the stairs, leading Candy without minding her. My little bellboy, she thought. Candy was a fan of motel rooms, not just the sleep-till-noon draperies and the little soaps but mostly the way she could be anybody she wanted to be in those blank rooms, or nobody at all, thinking of the scotch-and-TV seductions, the lonely salesmen who had laid their heads on the same pillow. A place to leave your life, be nobody for a while. The room that Walter left her in was a nobody room, a cold, clean little space over the stairway, back issues of *National Geographic,* a Bible and an antique pitcher-and-basin arrangement on top of the dresser with dried weeds sticking out of it. It was more like a bed-and-breakfast than a motel but the same feeling, the spotless carpeting and the virginal crisp sheets. Walter lit the bedside lamp, filling the room with pink light, and settled heavily on the end of the bed. "Do you want some company?" he whispered.

Candy started to laugh. "Have you been watching movies again?" she asked him. "Shouldn't you have a rose between your teeth?"

"Am I doing this wrong?"

"No," she said. "No, you're doing this just fine, I like it. I'm just not in the mood."

"For me?"

"For anyone. I'm sorry. And what if your mom found out? You might get grounded."

Walter got up from the bed, gave her a fuck-you look as he left the room. He would have slammed the door but he really was afraid to wake his mom up. Candy thought, OK, he's mad at me. She emptied one of the vases on the dresser of its faded dried flowers, wiped it clean with her handkerchief and rummaged through the depths of her suitcase until she found the dozen little airline bottles of brandy she left in there for emergencies. I declare this an emergency, she said to herself. Lit a

163

cigarette, the first one ever smoked in this room, and settled onto the bed and tried to read her mystery: the gun, the kiss, the trivial appointment. Somebody was about to be murdered or somebody had just been murdered, she couldn't remember. Really, she couldn't make heads or tails of it.

She went to the window and looked out to where the brothers were still draped around the picnic table, talking, though she couldn't hear them. Two thirds of a moon, enough to see by. There was the house, and the yard, and then nothing, a dark field as flat as a pool table. At the far edge of the field was a wall of ragged forest, with wild palm trees standing up against the sky, black on black. My love, she thought, my love is down there, and fairly soon he will come up to me. He will sing in my window. Then stopped herself, closed the curtain, went back to her lonely bed and her mystery. This is not appropriate, she thought. This is not wholesome. But the words on the page all turned to bugs and refused to be read. There was this thing called love and it would not leave her alone. The weight of it. An afternoon on a beach in Turkey, a flat expanse of sand. You could land a jet on it, Greg said. Then the limitless Mediterranean blue, islands on the horizon like dream kingdoms and the cold sun outlining every muscle of her husband's body, every grain of sand that clung to his skin like powdered sugar. Watching him as he lay eyes closed in the sand, an owner's pride in his body. Candy's sorrow was always mixed with desire: next to Greg in the sand, his sly hands, Turkish music from the Coca-Cola shops a hundred yards away, the blare of the tinny speakers hushed to almost nothing by the shore breeze and the surf. Nowhere to go, nowhere to hide, nobody else on the beach, but the sand was so flat that they could be seen for a quarter-mile; out of the question, but their apartment was an hour away. The girl she had been, when she was allowed that life: twenty, not beautiful but body-proud, ready to take risks. Greg pulling her toward the water, chest-deep in the Mediterranean, fumbling with her suit-bottom in distant sight of the Turkish families vacationing by the shore and then the feel of him inside her . . . and the weight of it, like water pouring down on her, and the sweetness. There were parts she was leaving out, she half-remembered them, but the sweetness was real.

She gave up on her mystery and poured another brandy for herself, two more, lining up the empty bottles like tiny rockets on the edge of the dresser. This night should be over soon. She would go to sleep, and in the morning she would be kind to Walter, and Jim would resemble nobody but himself. Her heart would not remember that it had ever woken up. Outside the window the cows were sleeping and the brothers were gone from the picnic table.

I will not stand for this, she thought.

Because she could still feel love inside her, like stitches pulling out. Because she had almost forgotten. Because she didn't want to think about her reasons anymore. Because she wanted to. Because Walter was such a reasonable man, although at the heart of things this had nothing to do with Walter. He was like a man you might see out the window of a moving train, but she spared him a moment's contempt as she brushed her hair out and smoothed her clothes: he was so safe! Safe as houses, she remembered. Greg loved to fly F-111s, almost twice the speed of sound.

Candy tiptoed down the carpeted stairs in her bare feet and shorts and he was still there in the kitchen, tipped back in his chair, drinking. When he noticed she was there, he aimed his glass at the screen of the television. "This is the most fucked-up movie I have ever seen," he said. "It's some sort of a pirate movie."

Candy squinted into the gray light of the screen, where a pair of oriental men in striped shirts were driving around in an ordinary motorboat. Even the music didn't make sense.

"Do you have any gin?" she asked.

"Around here someplace," he said, without taking his eyes from the screen. The two oriental men were still driving the boat. Then it occurred to Jim that he was called on to act, and he shook his head like he was waking up. "Gin," he said. "That would be like a gin and tonic, right? I'll round one up for you. Just stay where you are."

"Or a glass of wine," she said.

"That might be easier." He opened the refrigerator and stood there looking into the light, and it was quiet in the house, just the two of them. With Greg she was always moving, a series of one-bedroom apartments stacked like groceries. Their neighbors were always Air Force, just like them, but Candy and Greg had a plan, a future. Someday he was going to be a husband, getting his wife a glass of wine, standing in the refrigerator light . . . They had already decided not to have children till they were thirty-five. They were going to be selfish with their time. Thirty-five, she thought, next year.

Jim set a bottle of French wine on the table and started to wrestle it open. "I'm sure she was saving this for something," he said. "I'm sure we'll be in trouble in the morning but I'm in permanent trouble anyway."

"What about me?"

"Below the radar," Jim said. "Girlfriend of youngest son and favorite darling. You're about sixty percent threat and the rest pure evil."

"Well, that's reassuring," Candy said, taking a glass of wine from Jim's hand, easing into the chair next to him. Now there were two boats circling around each other and somebody was firing a machine gun and she was watching with her husband. Drinky logic, she reminded herself. Three in the morning. None of this was real. But why should that matter? If her own pleasure was real—and it was, the warmth of his presence, even the way he sat so restfully in his chair—then did it matter if she could prove it or not? This wasn't science.

She said, "The trouble is that I'm not tired at all."

"Be daylight in about two and a half more hours," he said. "The thing with cable—it's always daytime someplace. Only difference is they show the dirty movies in the night instead of the daytime."

"They do?"

"Oh yeah," he said. "It's a regular Sodom of the airwaves."

"Let's see," she said.

Jim looked at her sideways, and there was a moment when the whole thing hung in the balance. Candy had gone too far again, and again. And now was the time for him to turn into an adult and stop the game and make things safe again; she didn't know what to hope for but this was what she expected. Then it would be time for apologies, she thought, embarrassment, regret. Time for the heart to go to sleep again, the heart that was awake and restless, the heart out looking for something to do. Candy braced herself.

But he only grinned at her. "Shouldn't you be asleep?" he asked her.

"Shouldn't you be home?" she countered. But this drew blood. She saw him flinch a little, angry, and without another word he flicked the TV over to the skin channel. A couple of girls were naked in a garden, playing with each other's breasts and licking them. There was a lot of greenery and some running water and breathing. Funny-peculiar, Candy thought, not funny-hilarious. Is this what men want really? In the race between sex and ridiculous, ridiculous was clearly winning. That feels so good, the dark-haired girl said, don't stop. But what if your husband comes? asked the blonde. I don't care, the dark girl said, just suck me, suck me, suck me.

Ridiculous, Candy thought. At the same time, she was stirred by this fakery, down in her body. What if somebody was kissing her breasts right then? What if it was Jim? She thought of how good it would feel and thought of how lonely her body was and how much it wanted the touch of a man's hand, Jim's hand, and thought, That's about enough.

"OK," she said, "That's enough."

"This is the easy stuff," Jim said, glancing from the screen to her face and back to the screen. "You should see the shit they put on here sometimes, I mean dicks and everything."

He shut the TV off and the two sex girls disappeared to a little dot in the middle of the screen, then a brief flicker of light, like a ghost. In the sudden quiet she could hear the sounds of the night through the air-conditioning, the bugs and birds calling to each other. The loneliness of that mixed with the loneliness of her body. The thing was they were just calling out to the night, not to any one bug or any partner bird. They were just interchangeable, and this was where she felt the loneliness.

168

"I'm not tired at all," she said, though her own voice sounded tired in her ears. Big girl staying out past her bedtime. Something happens when you get tired, she remembered from childhood: the world starts to crumble, sand castles. And then Jim turned to her, and the cocky tilt of his head, the half-smile he gave her wasn't Jim at all but Greg, and she remembered what she was doing there.

"You want to go for a drive?" Jim asked.

"Sure I do," she said. "I've only been in the car for two and a half days."

"Does that mean yes or does that mean no?" he asked. "I can't tell with you."

"You can assume that I mean yes until further notice," she said, and then quickly, before he could think about that, she asked, "Do I need a jacket?"

"Not till November," he muttered, but he seemed distracted, like he was in a bad mood. And who could blame him? Sex and ridiculous, all at once, as she followed him out into the damp night. So much easier if she didn't think about it.

And then they were driving in a convertible with the top down, drinking cold beers from a cooler in the back, a big plush ride. Candy wondered how drunk he was, exactly. It didn't seem to matter. She wondered, if he crashed it, would she just wake up, or would she really be dead? And if she was dead, would she get to be twenty again, so she could be with Greg endlessly and perfectly with their perfect bodies . . . Everything was possible and nothing mattered. She could smoke as many cigarettes as she wanted to, if she could get them lit. They were following the headlights of the Buick down an endless straight zipper of a road that was elevated a few feet above the swamp. Off to the side Candy could see dark green and

dark water and sometimes eyes, glittering like jewels in the
night.

"You boys love your big cars," she said, the wind tearing
the words out of her mouth.

"Yes, ma'am, we do," Jim said, broadening his accent till
he sounded like a Beverly Hillbilly. "We sho'nuff do love our
big ole cars and our catfish and our Yankee cousins to tell us
what to do."

"I didn't mean anything."

"I know you didn't," Jim said. "I'm just an asshole."

"What's that out in the water there?"

"Alligators. That's how you find them, when you go hunting for them—shine a light across the water and look for the
eyes."

"Then what?" she asked.

"Stick him with a harpoon, let him run out a line till he get
tired of dragging the boat around, then hit him with a bang
stick—shotgun shell on the end of a pole, you let it go right
into his brain. See, it kills the brain but the rest of him don't
know it for a while. I was with a guy, he had a dead gator jump
all the way out of the boat when it was on the trailer going
back to the processing plant. Three guys trying to wrestle that
sonofabitch back into the boat by the side of the road with the
tail going back and forth and so on."

"Processing plant?"

"Where they do the hides and the skull and the gator
meat, you know. There's actually a fair amount of money in
it."

"Is that what you do it for?"

"No ma'am," he said in his hillbilly accent again. "I just do

170

it 'cause I have the gator blood in me. A man's born to it or he isn't and I was born to hunt gators."

"Serves me right," Candy said.

"Yes ma'am, it does," Jim said.

Just then he turned off the highway into a bumpy dirt lot, so fast that Candy wondered if they were having an accident. There was a sign up but it was dark and she couldn't read it. The big car bounced and heaved over the ruts and finally stopped at the side of a dirty white building. She saw beer signs in the window but they were all turned off. The paint was peeling off the building like a skin disease. Then he shut the headlights off.

Candy asked, "What are we doing here?"

"Junior's 99," he said, and leapt out of the car without opening the door.

Candy followed gingerly, looking all around her. A light was coming from somewhere, maybe the moon, enough to see the black water of the slough and the cypress trunks that rose out of it. There was a pickup truck in the parking lot but it looked like it had been there a decade. The building itself was patched with soda signs and propped with two-by-sixes to keep it from collapsing into the slough. There was a faint pink light coming out the dirty windows.

"I do not like this, Sam-I-am," Candy said. "What country are we in?"

"It's the 99 club," Jim said distractedly, as if he were reading it off a card. "Drink and dance and romance since 1943. Enjoy yourself."

He wandered through the door like he was moving underwater, and Candy followed him. The smell inside almost knocked her down: cat piss, cigars, wet paper, some odor of illness or death. She was surprised to find that she could see when she got inside: six or seven jukeboxes, a pool table, a rough wooden bar with five silver stools and an oyster-colored old man in a patched green BarcaLounger behind it. Above his head was the sign: WELCOME TO THE 99 CLUB   DRINK AND DANCE AND ROMANCE SINCE 1943   ENJOY YOURSELF.

"Slow night," Jim said.

The old man grunted, stared at Jim through his Coke-bottle glasses. As he got to his feet—sluggish, Candy thought, rusty—she saw that he had a dirty cast on his left arm. With his good hand he reached into a cooler behind the bar and brought out a couple of cold beers and set them dripping on the counter. "It's quarter to three in the goddamn morning," the old man said.

"Was it better before?" Jim asked.

"No." The old man went back to his seat and Jim opened the wet beers. No money changed hands. In the shadows at the end of the bar were three black men staring at them, not moving. The tips of their cigars glowed like fireflies in front of their dark faces, like the old men in Turkey—and again she found herself between the memory and the day, going with Greg into these scary places and trusting him, letting him do the thinking. Twenty-two years old, but she was still doing the same thing, except that she didn't know Jim enough to trust him. A little warning bell of danger went off in her head, and something else, a memory that wouldn't quite surface.

"What happens around here?" Candy asked. "What forms of recreation?"

"Pretty much what you see," Jim said. "Occasional dancing and livestock trading."

"What does that mean?"

"Just what I said." He fished in his pocket for change, ambled over to the jukebox, fed his quarters in and stood there glowing in the pink light, trying to decide. What did it mean when a man took his vices so seriously? Candy tried to think of her little apartment in Washington, D.C., tried to imagine that it was a safe place, but really it was no more meant for her than this. There was no place left for her. This seemed like such an evident thing that she couldn't see why the idea hadn't come to her before. Maybe she was sleepwalking, Candy thought. Maybe she was just going through the motions. She watched the man who was not her husband poking the buttons of the jukebox with a rough finger.

A record came on, scratched and rough, while he picked out a half-dozen more: *Sometimes I feel like crying, but the tears won't come down* . . . Then Jim ambled back over to Candy, everything slow, like underwater.

"I hope I didn't mislead you," he said, keeping his voice soft, down under the level of the jukebox so only she could hear. She could feel his breath on her neck. "I'm not the kindly one in this family," he said. "I'm sort of the black sheep, I guess."

He grinned at Candy and she smelled the whiskey on his breath, and the complicated stench of the bar, and it was like being on the back of a motorcycle, not even driving, and feeling the push of the big motor and knowing that it didn't matter, somebody else was driving, too late for her desires to make a difference . . .

"I'm sorry," she said. "I wish . . ."

"What's that?" he asked.

But she didn't know how she was going to end that sentence, and so she improvised: "It's just so close in here, you know? I don't know. Maybe if we went outside."

Jim looked at her, and maybe Candy would have seen something if she'd been a little more front-and-center. But she was thinking, dreaming: if wishes were horses . . . This one fall day when they were down in Virginia riding through the mountains on Greg's bike, down to look at the leaves. It was cold in the shadows and warm in the sun, riding down miles of white board fences, with the horses scattered across the grass and the hills in all the shades of brown and orange and yellow, like a beggar's coat. Candy clung to Greg's back as they swung through the corners, faster and faster, not even scared after a while—no helmets, not then, just the wind in her face and the whine of the beat-up Kawasaki 500 and the kick when they came around a corner and Greg hit the throttle and the road-side weeds melted into a blur of speed, the tire trembling underneath her. And then leaning through one corner she saw the slick of wet leaves at the same time Greg did, too late, and she felt the rear tire slip out from under her and then the front and they were going for the guardrail and she hung on tight like he could save her, the bike fishtailing back through center and off the wrong way and then back through, by some accident, so the bike was at the right angle when it hit the gravel shoulder and they slid sideways and they didn't even fall down, not all the way. Greg didn't bother to shut the engine down. He just sat there on the bike staring down the road, with Candy on his back like a limpet, and then after a minute he started to laugh. He turned his head so Candy could kiss his cheek and she did. She was still too afraid to move and he was laughing, gunning the engine back to life. Even then it didn't make any sense. It was just love in the pure form, there wasn't any reasonability to it but just the pure longing in the belly and in the throat. They almost died and he was laughing, and Candy wept as they rode away, partly from the wind, partly out of pure love. The ride and then the warm apartment at the end of it and the leaves and horses.

There was something in there, something Candy wanted to think about, couldn't quite get hold of, about women and men and adventures: how it seemed as if women always got smaller in adventure, how they gave themselves away, while men only got bigger . . . There was something else missing, too, some piece of the puzzle. If only she had a minute she could make sense out of it, but Jim was leading her back out into the night. This was where things started to move too fast. She started to want a break, just to sit down somewhere and untangle things, even just to tell how drunk she was, which wasn't clear.

Outside was the same pink light and stink, and the music was echoing through the cypress trees from speakers out of sight. Jim led her along the water on an old cracked concrete walkway, with a railing made of plumbing. Decayed amusement: broken Christmas lights strung from the trees, jagged in their bases. Candy wondered, Why do red and green and blue and yellow all together add up to pink? Behind the roadhouse stood a wall of pine trees. Jim led her toward a lattice-work gate and inside.

"The whispering pines," he said. The trees made a dark circle all around them, and then there was a circle of lights, strung from pole to pole and most of them still working, and then in the center of everything was the dance floor. It was made out of wood, raised three or four feet off the ground, with railing around the outside and a pavilion in the middle.

Once it had been painted white but the paint was chipping or mildew-stained or mossy green. The sound of the jukebox was louder here, coming out of cone-shaped PA speakers like the kind in junior high school or prison, as if the sound were being squeezed through some kind of metal tube, Candy thought. Eventual headache, loud as it was. Jim said, "Let's dance, you want to?"

"I don't usually," Candy said.

"Make an exception for me, just this time. Come on."

He took her wrist and led her up the stairs, out onto the plywood floor. It was treacherous footing. Nails had come up through the edges, and rain had warped the plywood so the individual sheets no longer fit together right: there were gaps, and little steps. The framework underneath her creaked and groaned as she walked, and her heels made a drumming sound against the hollow space below, so that it was like walking across a large musical instrument. Out of the speaker cones she heard the tick and pop of a new record, and then the hiss gave way to an easy, loping beat, to Al Green's—but this time not the Reverend, this time it was the old, sexy Al Green singing, *I don't know why I love you like I do . . .*

Jim started to sway his hips in time to the music, an awkward, stilted white-boy dance, but he didn't seem to care. He grinned at her. "Come on," he said. "Come on, baby."

The dance floor drummed and shook like it was about to shake itself to pieces and Candy saw the headline, NORTHERN STRANGER DIES IN DANCE FLOOR CATASTROPHE, but he was dancing and she wanted to. She stepped carefully over, so they'd be on the same sheet of plywood and wouldn't trip, and she started to do the only dances she knew, the ones from high school, the Frug and the Philly Jerk and the James Brown. Candy waved her arms in the air like a crazy woman. Jim saw her. He shook his hips and he waved his arms and he looked up at the lights, so the pink and yellow hit him full in the face, and he closed his eyes, still dancing, and in that moment the time got strange and Candy got lost, spinning back through the years to high school and nothing was real, nothing existed but this, this boy in her arms, Greg waving his arms in the air . . .

Candy collapsed against Jim's chest, crying. The record went on playing. He let her stay there for a second, but then he extricated himself and stood at arm's length.

"What's the matter with you?" he asked her. "Everything was going along just fine and then all of a sudden . . ."

Jim was angry, but this was just one more fact she couldn't understand then. She'd seen her husband, the way he showed himself in dreams, her lover, her boy, and in his eyes she saw the girl she once used to be, and that girl was just as dead as Greg was. Poor Candy, she thought, Candy's dead, poor Candy. It was like a jingle or a nursery rhyme and she couldn't get it out of her head. There was life between them and love and then sorrow when he died, but Candy saw, standing on the dance floor, that sorrow had turned into nothing more than a habit. She was just a shell, an empty place where something had once happened, like a battlefield—the miles of empty lawns, well kept. There was nowhere to go from here. She could walk off in the woods and just lie down, one of those unsolved cases. Candy thought of what that would be like— she thought of what the rain would sound like, the first drops filtering through the trees, hitting the leaves by her ears. She saw herself lying there. If she stayed unfound the leaves would grow up through her chest, through her ribs, a little empty cave of bones. Candy imagined that she could feel them. Poor Candy, she thought. Candy's dead.

She barely noticed when Jim led her off the dance floor, into the darkness of the little pavilion. When he started kissing her it was like something in a dream, the inevitable surprise. Here in the dark it was easy to pretend. She let her mind go out of focus, let go, let it slip past her. But when she felt the stranger's tongue in her mouth, he was suddenly real, and all wrong.

"Hold on a minute," she said, and tried to edge away.

But he only held her tighter with the arm that was around her waist, his other hand up the front of her blouse now. She felt his size and his strength against her and she was afraid. A cold sweat broke out on her back, and she shivered under his hand, seeing what a fool she had been. At the same time, the beginnings of anger: why was she always the one who had to pay?

"Look, I know," she said, "I may have said something or done something . . ."

"That isn't how it works," he said.

"What?"

"You may tease somebody but you aren't going to tease me," he said. He was standing back from her and she could just see the side of his face in the pink light and he seemed entirely calm, as if he were explaining some elementary fact to a young child. "There's different kinds of people in this world, and I'm one of them," he said. "You can fuck around with Walter all you want to."

"Fred C. Dobbs," she said. "1948."

"What?"

"You just remind me of somebody," she said. "I'm sorry, but I think we ought to go."

"That isn't how it works," he said again, and this time he took her hand and pressed it to the front of his chinos so she could feel his erection through the thin material. It was a long, skinny thing, like a dog's, Candy thought, and a little shiver ran through her. He pressed her down with his hand until she knelt in front of him. Childhood prayers raced stupidly through her thoughts: Hail Mary, full of grace, the Lord is with thee . . . She opened his belt and then the zipper and worked his pants down over his knees, stopping to take his shoes off, one after the other.

"You don't have to do that," Jim said.

"No, but I want to," Candy said, and slipped his pants off over his stockinged feet. Her hands went to his waist, and she slowly slid his underwear down his thighs, little-boy under-wear, white Jockey shorts with the little stripe around the waistband, nothing to fear from his underwear. His penis was ridiculous, too, standing up like a crooked mushroom, a little off to one side. When his shorts were down around his ankles, Candy grabbed his pants and took off running.

"What the fuck?" Jim shouted. "Get the fuck over here."

The jukebox was playing loud as ever as Candy wobbled across the dance floor, not wanting to look back: if he was going to catch her she didn't want to know. As she ran she fumbled in the pockets, and found his keys at the same time she left the circle of pines, running along the stagnant creek on the broken walkway. The fear was all on the surface of her mind but underneath was calm, like she knew what to do. She threw the pants over the rail into the water and ran through the pink light past the bar, escaping. Not until she was in the car with the motor going did she look behind her: nothing, and then she saw him at the edge of the lights, his white legs shining. "Bitch!" he was shouting. "Bitch!"

She lowered the shifter into Drive and sprayed gravel out of the parking lot, trailing one arm out the window with the middle finger up. She knew it was bad luck but she didn't care. She was out of bad luck anyway. The calm was on her again, and then the thing that she had been trying to remember, or maybe trying to forget, came back to her: an evening in her apartment, two or three months after the funeral, and coming home to find it empty and cold as always and standing alone in her good wool coat in the living room, before she turned the lights on, and wondering, What do I do now? What do I want to do? And now, escaping—this is really a stolen car, she thought, I've never done this before—she remembered the strange taste it left in her mouth, the power of it, the witchy woman. She was past love and past death and they couldn't touch her. Candy shivered in the hot night, remembering. Something she wanted. What did she want now? This was the hidden thing. I don't want anything, really, none for me, the polite nonentity. Fuck it, Candy thought. She reached into the back for one of Greg's cold beers and opened it and pointed the big soft car toward Sarasota and took off, fast.

about the author

KEVIN CANTY'S STORIES HAVE BEEN PUBLISHED IN *ESQUIRE* AND in *Story* magazine, among other places. He lives in Montana, where he is at work on a novel, the opening chapters of which won a *TransAtlantic Review* award from the Henfield Foundation.